The War of the Words

"Jessica," Elizabeth said, in a low voice, "putting out a newspaper takes a lot of work. Besides, there's probably not room for *two* newspapers at this school."

Jessica gave a short laugh. "That's really what you're afraid of, isn't it, Elizabeth? You're afraid that our newspaper will be so good that nobody will want to read yours."

"No, I'm not," Elizabeth replied, starting to get angry again. "I just don't want you to go to a lot of work just to make me mad!"

"Oh, Elizabeth, don't worry about that!" She turned away from her twin and waved at Lila and Ellen. "Now, if you'll excuse me, I've got to go. The Unicorns are having a meeting this afternoon to organize our first edition, and I don't want to be late." She started to go, then turned back. "Oh, and thank you for rejecting my article," she said in a nasty voice. "If it hadn't been for you, I might never have gotten my brilliant idea!"

Elizabeth watched as Jessica walked away with her friends. *If that's the way you feel, Jessica,* she said to herself, *then the battle of the newspapers is on!*

Bantam Skylark Books in the SWEET VALLEY TWINS series
Ask your bookseller for the books you have missed

SWEET VALLEY TWINS

The War Between the Twins

Written by
Jamie Suzanne

Created by
FRANCINE PASCAL

A BANTAM SKYLARK BOOK®
NEW YORK · TORONTO · LONDON · SYDNEY · AUCKLAND

RL 4, 008-012

THE WAR BETWEEN THE TWINS
A Bantam Skylark Book / March 1990

*Skylark Books is a registered trademark of Bantam Books,
a division of Bantam Doubleday Dell Publishing Group, Inc.
Registered in U.S. Patent and Trademark Office and elsewhere.*

*Sweet Valley High® and Sweet Valley Twins are
trademarks of Francine Pascal.*

Conceived by Francine Pascal.

*Produced by Daniel Weiss Associates, Inc.,
33 West 17th Street, New York, NY 10011*

Cover art by James Mathewuse.

ISBN 0-553-15779-5

Published simultaneously in the United States and Canada

*Bantam Books are published by Bantam Books, a division of Bantam
Doubleday Dell Publishing Group, Inc. Its trademark, consisting of the
words "Bantam Books" and the portrayal of a rooster, is Registered in
U.S. Patent and Trademark Office and in other countries. Marca Regis-
trada. Bantam Books, 666 Fifth Avenue, New York, New York 10103.*

PRINTED IN THE UNITED STATES OF AMERICA

OPM   0 9 8 7 6 5 4

For Susan Kitzen and Elise Howard

One

◇

"Here it is, Lizzie," Jessica announced proudly as she put a piece of paper down on the desk in front of her identical twin sister, Elizabeth.

Elizabeth looked up from her homework. "Hmmm," she murmured, with an exaggerated look of concentration. "What could this be?" She bit her bottom lip to keep herself from smiling.

Jessica wasn't fooled. "You know very well what it is," she said smugly. "It's my Unicorn story for the *Sixers*. And it's a *very good* story. In fact, it's the best thing I've ever written." A concerned look suddenly passed over Jessica's face. "You haven't forgotten your promise, have you?"

Elizabeth wasn't quite finished teasing her twin yet. "My promise?" she asked, mimicking the look on her sister's face. "Did I promise you anything?"

It was easy for Elizabeth to imitate Jessica. Both girls had the same long blond hair and blue-green eyes. In fact, they looked so much alike that strangers could not tell them apart. Only the twins' family and closest friends knew how to tell them apart, and even they got confused at times. One of the easiest ways to tell which twin was which was to look at what they were wearing. Jessica wore something purple almost every day because she was a member of the exclusive Unicorn Club. The Unicorns *always* wore something purple—the color of royalty—to show how special and unique they were, and they made sure to dress in the most current fashions. Jessica took special care choosing her clothes and wore her hair in loose waves around her face. She was confident that she looked much more sophisticated than most of the other girls in school.

Elizabeth was not a member of the Unicorn Club. She had been invited to join, but as she sat in her first meeting listening to Jessica and her friends talk about boys, clothes, and makeup, she realized there were lots of places she would rather be. In fact, she invented a new name for the club which she thought suited them perfectly: the Snob

Squad. Elizabeth's favorite activity was working on the *Sweet Valley Sixers*, the sixth-grade newspaper that she had helped to found. Elizabeth hoped to be a writer some day, and she knew that working on the school newspaper would give her some valuable experience.

"Lizzie," Jessica said, a note of warning in her voice.

Elizabeth picked up the piece of paper. "OK, OK, Jess. Of course I remember my promise," she said. "I promised that your story would appear in the very next issue of the *Sixers*. Right?"

"Right," Jessica said firmly. "And not a minute later. The Unicorns are getting ready to clobber you." For weeks, Jessica and the Unicorns had been complaining that the newspaper wasn't paying enough attention to their club.

Elizabeth sighed. If she'd heard one complaint about the *Sixers* from Jessica and the Unicorns, she'd heard a hundred. Suddenly, she was feeling very serious. "I don't know why they'd want to clobber *me*," she said.

Jessica rolled her eyes. "Because you're the one who keeps leaving us out of the paper," she explained.

"That's not true," Elizabeth said quietly. It *was* true that there had not been anything about the club in the *Sixers* since their last fund-raising event months before. But there was a good reason for leaving them out, as far as Elizabeth was concerned. The Unicorns never did anything that was really worth writing about.

"I still think that if you wanted to put us in, you could," Jessica said. "It's not as if we don't do anything exciting. Ellen Riteman went to Santa Monica for a whole weekend. Then there was that great shopping trip to the mall, not to mention the letter that Lila Fowler got from the Donny Diamond Fan Club! I mean," she added, "Donny Diamond is *only* the most popular teen rock star in the entire U.S.A."

Elizabeth took a deep breath. They had been through this many times before, and each time she had pointed out that no one would be interested in someone else's shopping trip or a letter from a fan club to which they didn't belong. Finally, she had decided to let Jessica write a short article updating all the latest Unicorn news. Jessica could write about the shopping trip or Lila's letter or anything else. The only catch was that she had to keep it down to two hundred words.

"I have to tell you," Jessica said, pointing to the paper in Elizabeth's hand, "it was almost impossible to cram everything into just two hundred words. But I did it," she said proudly.

Writing a story that included all the Unicorns' special news was a job that Jessica had taken very seriously. She had spent days gathering the information, writing it, rewriting it, and checking it with her friends so nobody felt neglected. Mary Wallace, a fellow Unicorn, helped by typing it for her. Jessica intended to make sure that her twin put it into the *Sixers* exactly as she had written it. She felt it was such a masterpiece that it would be a shame if Elizabeth decided to change even a single word.

"Do you think you could put my story on the front page?" she added. "It's definitely good enough to be the lead story."

"I promise," Elizabeth said, "that it will be in the very next issue. But I *can't* promise that it will go on the front page." She got out her backpack and tucked the story safely inside while Jessica watched. "We'll be typing up the ditto master for the paper during lunch tomorrow. So you'll see your article when the paper comes out the day after that."

At lunch the next day, the Unicorns had gathered around Jessica to read a copy of her story. Everybody loved it.

"I see," Lila Fowler said, "that you've included something about the letter I got from the

Donny Diamond Fan Club." She looked pleased. "I know people will be interested in reading about that."

Ellen Riteman smiled at Jessica. "I like what you say about my trip to Santa Monica. You're absolutely right, it *was* fabulous."

"I think," Janet Howell said, "you did an excellent job, Jessica." Janet was the president of the Unicorns and an eighth-grader. Jessica thought Janet was one of the most important girls in the middle school, and she was very pleased to have made a good impression on her. "I especially liked the part about the dance. I think everybody should know that the president of the Unicorns has been put in charge of the dance." She looked around the group. "If people know the Unicorns are in charge, they'll definitely want to come."

"You know, Jessica," Janet continued, "I think you should tell Elizabeth that it would be an excellent idea if you wrote a Unicorn story for the *Sixers* once a month."

Jessica was relieved when Janet was interrupted by the bell signaling the end of the lunch hour. She had had a hard enough time getting Elizabeth to agree to print *one* article. She didn't even want to think about asking Elizabeth to print one a month.

"Maybe you could come over to my house tonight," Lila said, turning to Janet. "Jessica and Ellen are coming over to work on a social studies project. We could have a meeting—that would give us plenty of time to talk about the dance and to discuss topics for more Unicorn articles."

Janet smiled. "Sounds great!" she said, glancing around the group. "Everybody, come to Lila's house tonight at seven for a mandatory meeting. We have a lot to discuss."

"Mandatory?" Jessica whispered to Mary Wallace.

"That means we all have to go," Mary explained.

"Oh," Jessica said with a grin. "I wouldn't mind if all of the Unicorn meetings were mandatory!"

"This is impossible," Julie Porter muttered.

Elizabeth looked up from her work and made a face at her friend. "You can say that again!" she said.

Julie and Elizabeth were having a difficult time. The lunch hour was half over, and they were trying to finish the ditto masters for the next issue of the *Sixers*. It was due out the next day. The problem was there was so much important news that they had had a hard time fitting everything onto each page.

"Why does it always work out this way?" Julie asked. "One week nothing happens, and the next week too much happens!"

Unfortunately, Elizabeth thought to herself, *there isn't a single story we can leave out.* Jessica's piece was the least important—not only because most of the items in it were of interest only to the Unicorns, but also because most of it was old news. The trip to the shopping mall had taken place weeks before, and Ellen's visit to Santa Monica had been at least two months ago. But Elizabeth did not even consider leaving Jessica's article out. She had made a promise and she was going to stick to it.

"Julie," Elizabeth said, "if anyone can do it, we can!" She gave her friend the thumbs-up sign. "Now, let's get back to work!"

Julie gave Elizabeth a mock salute. "OK, chief," she said, giggling.

The girls worked quietly for several more minutes.

When she was done, Julie pushed her chair back and pulled the ditto master she had been working on out of her typewriter. "I can't believe it," she said, turning to Elizabeth, "but it's all in here. How are you doing?"

Elizabeth grinned and typed the final period on her ditto. "Finished!" she exclaimed triumphantly. She glanced at her watch. "And just in time, too. I think we can get the first page run off before the bell rings." She got up and turned on the ditto machine. "Hand me that first page, Julie, and I'll just—"

"Stop the presses!" Mr. Bowman called out, coming into the room. Mr. Bowman taught sixth-grade English. He was also the faculty supervisor for the *Sixers.* His students liked to tease him behind his back because he never wore clothes that coordinated. Today, for instance, he was wearing a pink pin-striped shirt with a yellow and green polka-dot bow tie. He usually looked silly, but he had a big heart, a great sense of humor, and was well-liked by all the students.

"Hi, Mr. Bowman," Elizabeth said, turning off the ditto-machine switch. He was her favorite teacher. "What's up?"

"Bad news, girls," Mr. Bowman said in a glum voice. "Coach Cassels broke his leg playing football in the park yesterday evening. It seems he'll be in the hospital for a few weeks."

"Oh, that's too bad," Elizabeth said. Julie, who looked very serious, nodded. "What's going to happen to the basketball team?" she asked.

Mr. Bowman smiled at Julie. "I don't know," he told her, "but that is an excellent question. It's just the sort of information that belongs on the front page of the paper. What do you think, girls? Everybody will want to know that Coach Cassels is in the hospital."

Julie glanced quickly at Elizabeth. "Uh-oh," she said half under her breath.

Elizabeth frowned. *Another* story? The paper was already crammed full. There wasn't enough room to put in one more word without taking out something else. And there wasn't anything she could take out.

"I don't know . . ." Elizabeth began doubtfully. But then she stopped herself. The news about Coach Cassels going into the hospital was very important. More important, in fact, than any other story that was in the paper. There was no doubt about what she had to do.

"Sorry, Julie," Elizabeth said. "It looks like we've got some more work to do before we can run the front page."

Mr. Bowman smiled. "Well," he said, "I guess

we'd better get to work!" He turned toward the door. "I think someone should go down to the principal's office and find out what Mrs. Knight knows." Mrs. Knight was the principal's secretary. "Since this is a special circumstance, I'll let Amy Sutton write up the story during my class this afternoon."

After Mr. Bowman left, Julie looked at Elizabeth with a defeated expression. "What are we going to *do*?" she said. "There isn't room for another story unless we take something out. And the *Sixers* is always six pages long."

There was a long silence while they both looked at the pages they had typed.

"Maybe we could take out the piece about the art show," Julie suggested.

"We can't do that," Elizabeth said. "The winners deserve to see their names in the paper."

"Well, then, what about the interview with the student-council president? We could run it next week."

Elizabeth shook her head. "It's important for everybody to know what the president is planning," she replied. She bit her lip. "I'm afraid that the Unicorns will have to wait until next week to see their names in the paper."

Julie's eyes widened. "If you kill Jessica's story . . ." She paused. "Jessica might kill you! In fact, *all* of the Unicorns will be after you."

Elizabeth sighed. "Jessica *will* be very upset," she told her friend, "but I think she'll understand." *I hope she'll understand*, she added to herself.

Two

◇

Three minutes past five, Elizabeth noted, glancing at the clock in the den. "Jessica sure is late today," she said to her mother.

All afternoon, Elizabeth had been dreading telling Jessica that her article would not appear until the following week. But she couldn't put it off. The newspaper would be out first thing in the morning.

Mrs. Wakefield looked up from the magazine she was reading. "Don't you remember, Liz?" she asked. "Jessica's spending the night at Lila's house. They're working on their social studies project."

Now Elizabeth felt really worried. If Jessica was not coming home that evening, she couldn't tell her the news.

"What's the matter, Elizabeth?" Mrs. Wakefield asked, noticing her daughter's worried look.

"I have to tell Jessica something important," Elizabeth replied.

"Why don't you call her over at Lila's?" Mrs. Wakefield suggested.

Elizabeth shook her head. "I don't think so, Mom," she said. She didn't want to tell Jessica about the article over the telephone. It was something she thought she had better tell her face-to-face.

"Maybe you're right, honey," Mrs. Wakefield said. "Jessica is probably busy with that social studies project. It might be better to wait until tomorrow morning."

"Thanks, Mom," Elizabeth said. She wandered out of the den, deep in thought. *Tomorrow morning*, Elizabeth decided, *I'll get to school extra early, distribute the papers, and then wait for Jessica by the front door. I'll just have to wait until then to tell her.*

"All right," Janet Howell said in her best president's voice. "Let's see if everyone knows what they're supposed to do. Kimberly?"

"Decorations," Kimberly answered.

"Ellen?"

"Refreshments."

"Tamara?"

"Publicity."

"Jessica?"

"Help Tamara with publicity."

"That's because you did such a super job getting the Unicorns' article into the *Sixers*," Janet told Jessica. "Lila?"

"Music."

"Good," Janet went on. "Everyone knows what she's supposed to do. Now, I want you all to get other people, not Unicorns, to serve on your committees. That way," she continued importantly, "nobody can accuse the Unicorns of trying to steal the spotlight."

"Great idea!" Tamara said with a smile. "I think I'll ask Bruce Patman to help Jessica and me with publicity."

"All right!" Jessica exclaimed. Jessica had a crush on Bruce. Even though he was conceited, most of the Unicorns thought he was the cutest boy in the seventh grade.

"You can have Bruce," Lila said, making a face. "I'm going to ask Rick Hunter," she added triumphantly. Rick was a handsome seventh-grader. Everybody liked him. "I'm sure Rick and I will find a great band."

"Now, Lila," Janet said. "Remember that the

music will be all-important. The student bands are OK, but everybody's heard them a dozen times. I want your committee to come up with something really new and exciting."

"Oh, we will," Lila said confidently. "You can count on us."

"Well, since that's settled, I guess we're done," Janet said, standing up. She gave Jessica an approving smile. "I don't usually read the *Sixers*, of course, but I'm looking forward to seeing your Unicorn article in print. I'll get a copy first thing when I get to school tomorrow."

Jessica felt very pleased with herself. It was wonderful to have friends who were so interested in her writing, she thought happily.

"Now," Lila said to Jessica and Ellen as she came back into her room after showing the rest of the Unicorns to the door, "we have about a half hour before we have to go to bed. That should be enough time to work on our social studies project, right?"

"Oh," Jessica agreed, "more than enough time!"

The next morning, Jessica got up and carefully smoothed out her white miniskirt and purple T-shirt. It was her favorite outfit. Today was the day when *everybody* would read her article, and she wanted to look her best when she received their compliments.

"Come on! We're going to be late," Lila said over and over, but Jessica refused to be hurried. She wanted to make sure that she looked perfect. By the time Jessica was ready to go, Lila decided it was too late for them to walk to school. Luckily her father was on his way to the office, and he offered to drive them.

He dropped them off at the back door. "We're here," Ellen grumbled as they climbed out of the car. "Finally."

But Jessica didn't even realize that Ellen was complaining. Happily, she hurried up the stairs. Jessica couldn't *wait* to get to homeroom and read her newspaper article!

"Where can she be?" Elizabeth asked Amy as she anxiously watched the crowd coming through the front door of Sweet Valley Middle School. Elizabeth had explained to Amy how important it was for her to find Jessica before homeroom. They had been waiting in the front hallway of the school for over twenty minutes, but Jessica was nowhere to be seen.

"Maybe we should wait in front of homeroom," Amy said. "That way you can't miss her."

Elizabeth sighed. "I just thought that if I could catch her *before* she got to homeroom, I could talk to her alone. I don't want to tell her in front of Lila and Ellen." Jessica was going to be upset, Elizabeth knew, and it would be easier for her if she was not embarrassed in front of her friends. "Let's wait a few more minutes."

"No problem," Amy said cheerfully. She looked at her watch. "We still have ten minutes until the bell."

But one minute went by, then two, then three, and there was no sign of Jessica. Finally, Elizabeth and Amy turned to walk down the hallway to their homeroom.

Suddenly, Amy grabbed Elizabeth's arm. "There she is!" she exclaimed, pointing toward the end of the hall. "She's with Lila and Ellen. They're going into homeroom!"

Elizabeth knew they were not supposed to run in the halls, but there was no rule against walking fast. With Amy at her heels, she took a deep breath and hurried down the hall. Maybe she could catch up with Jessica before she got to the newspapers lying just inside Mr. Davis's door.

But as soon as she got into her homeroom, she saw that Jessica already had a newspaper. And she could tell by the surprise and dismay on her twin's face that she was too late.

"I don't understand!" Ellen wailed, waving the paper. "Where is it?"

"Wherever it is," Lila said, sounding very annoyed, "it's not here."

Jessica leafed through the paper again, searching frantically. "We must have missed it," she said. "Maybe a page was left out when they stapled it. Or maybe this is an old paper."

"All the pages are in order," Lila said. "And it's today's paper, all right and we *didn't* miss it." She scowled at Jessica. "I thought you said Elizabeth promised to put it in this week's issue."

"She did," Jessica said angrily. Her throat was beginning to ache with disappointment. "I can't believe this is happening!"

"I think Elizabeth did this on purpose," Lila said. "She did it because she wanted to embarrass us. Jessica, I think it's time you did something about your sister. She left it out because she doesn't like the Unicorns!"

"Oh, I don't think Elizabeth—" Jessica began, instinctively ready to come to her twin's defense. But then Jessica stopped. All the evidence she needed was the paper in her hand. The article was not in it. And that could only mean one thing: Elizabeth had decided to leave it out. Jessica's disappointment was quickly giving way to anger. She had counted on Elizabeth to keep her promise. She had trusted her. And Elizabeth had let her down. She had made her look foolish in front of Lila and Ellen and all the other Unicorns who were expecting to see their names in the paper. Jessica's face turned bright red as she imagined Janet Howell picking up the paper to read the news about the dance. What was *Janet* going to say?

Suddenly Lila nudged her. "There's Elizabeth," she hissed. "Go talk to her."

Jessica looked up. Elizabeth had just entered the room and was hurrying over to them.

"Jessica," Elizabeth said breathlessly, "I want to talk to you about—"

Jessica pulled herself up straight, narrowing her eyes. "About breaking your promise?" she asked in a cold, strong voice. Lila and Ellen stood behind her with their arms crossed, with scowls on their faces.

Elizabeth looked at Jessica. Jessica had seen that look before, and she recognized it as Elizabeth's *guilty* look. That look convinced her that Elizabeth had meant to leave the article out. Jessica was growing angrier and angrier by the second.

How *dare* Elizabeth do such a thing? It was an insult to her and to all the Unicorns!

"I know what you must think," Elizabeth said in a low voice. "I'm sorry about your article. But I can explain. You see, Coach Cassels—"

"You're going to blame this on poor Coach Cassels," Lila interrupted bitterly. "It says right here on the front page of *your* paper that he's in the hospital! What could *he* have to do with this?"

Jessica put her hands on her hips. "Really, Elizabeth," she said indignantly, "you ought to be ashamed of yourself. Can't you come up with a better excuse than that?"

"It's *not* an excuse," Elizabeth protested. *Why can't Jessica listen for once?* she thought. "It's the truth! There was so much news that we just couldn't fit your article in."

"You mean, you didn't *want* to fit it in," Jessica said. "Admit it, Elizabeth, you've never liked the Unicorns. You've left us out of your stupid newspaper all year, and now you're leaving us out again!" Jessica stepped closer to Elizabeth until they were standing eye to eye. She glared at her sister. "Don't even try to lie to us, Elizabeth. We know you did this on purpose!"

"Jessica, you're wrong," Elizabeth said. She was trying to stay calm, but she was so upset her voice was beginning to shake. *How could Jessica call me a liar?* she thought furiously. "I haven't left you out of the paper all year. And I didn't leave your story out on purpose," she continued, "but it just wasn't that important in comparison to the other news we had to fit in."

Immediately, Elizabeth saw that she'd said the wrong thing. Jessica's eyes began to blaze. "Not that important?" she cried. "Did you just say my article wasn't that important?"

Jessica looked so angry, Elizabeth was almost afraid. "I'm sorry, Jessica, but I had no choice," she said, speaking in a whisper.

Elizabeth's calm only made Jessica angrier. "You can't get away with this, Elizabeth Wakefield!" she yelled.

That did it. Now Elizabeth was angry. "I never tried to get away with anything," she said, beginning to shout. She didn't care that there were people standing around listening to every word they were saying. She was so angry she didn't care who heard them fight. "Why don't you just listen to the facts?"

"Who cares about your stupid *facts!*" Jessica yelled back. She leaned forward and shook her finger at Elizabeth. "You think you can leave people out and they can't do a thing about it." She straightened up and tossed her hair over her shoulder. "I'll show you, Elizabeth."

Elizabeth folded her arms and lifted her chin. "Oh, yes?" she asked in a tone that she knew would only infuriate Jessica more.

But instead, Jessica smiled. An idea had occurred to her, an idea so brilliant, so absolutely *perfect* that it almost took her breath away.

"You know, Elizabeth," she said smugly. "You're not the only one who can run a newspaper. The Unicorns are going to start one, too. And our newspaper is going to be a hundred times better than yours!"

"That's what *you* think," Elizabeth said, holding her head high. If Jessica thought she was going to start up a newspaper, she had a lot of hard times ahead of her.

"Yes, that's *exactly* what I think," Jessica retorted. "And, for starters, you can just give me back my *unimportant* article," she said. "It's going to be the lead story in the first edition of the Unicorn newspaper!"

Three

◇

"Jessica," Ellen said breathlessly, as the girls slid into their seats, "you were *wonderful*! What a terrific idea!"

Lila's eyes shone. "You were really fabulous," she told Jessica. "I can't believe we never thought of having our own newspaper until now. It's perfect!"

Jessica gave her friends a modest smile. "I think it's the *only* solution," she said. "If Elizabeth doesn't think our news is good enough, we'll print it ourselves."

As Mr. Davis began to call roll, Jessica sat back in her chair, remembering the look of shock on her sister's face. Elizabeth was so stupid! She never expected that anybody—much less her very own twin—would challenge the *Sixers* by putting out another newspaper. And if the Unicorns' newspaper was good it might replace the *Sixers* entirely!

For a moment, Jessica felt a twinge of regret. Elizabeth really cared about the *Sixers*. She would be very hurt if everybody chose to read the Unicorns' newspaper instead.

But Jessica's discomfort vanished when she thought about what Elizabeth had done. Maybe a little competition would be good for Elizabeth. In fact, it might teach her a lesson.

On the other side of the room, Elizabeth and Amy took their seats.

"Elizabeth," Amy said in a low whisper, "I've never seen you and Jessica get so mad at each other."

Elizabeth sighed. Even though it was only the first class of the day, she felt exhausted. She hated to lose her temper. She knew that getting angry at Jessica never helped. And this time it had probably made things a lot worse.

"Do you think Jessica really means it?" Amy added. "About starting another newspaper, I mean."

Elizabeth shook her head. "She can try," she

said. "Publishing a newspaper takes a lot of work. It just might teach her a lesson!"

Amy laughed. "I just can't see Jessica slaving over the ditto machine. And can you imagine Lila and Ellen spending hours putting the pages in order and stapling them together? They'll give up the idea when they realize how much work is involved," she added, settling into her seat.

But as Elizabeth took out her notebook and began to look through the day's assignments, she felt a bit worried. Jessica had been hurt by what had happened. To make matters worse, Lila and Ellen had been hanging on to every word of the twins' argument. They would probably think it was a great idea for the Unicorns to start their own paper.

How did all this begin? And where is it going to end? Elizabeth wondered.

"Jessica, I want to talk to you," Janet Howell announced as she sat down at the usual Unicorn lunch table. "I want you to know that I am very disappointed that your article didn't appear in the *Sixers* today."

Jessica's heart sank.

"Of course," Janet continued, "I realize it's not your fault. We have your sister, Elizabeth, to thank for this disaster. Sometimes I find it hard to believe that the two of you are sisters. Anyway, I'm almost glad it happened—since it gave you such a brilliant idea. I think having a Unicorn newspaper will be great!"

Jessica let out a sigh of relief. *The news sure traveled fast,* she thought to herself.

"How did you think of it?" Tamara Chase asked.

"It was just one of those things," Jessica said casually, as if she came up with a brilliant idea every hour or so. "It just popped into my head. It felt like the only thing to do."

"The best part about Jessica's idea is that *we* can control the news," Janet explained. "We can write about anything we want." She glanced around the table.

"That's right," Ellen Riteman said. "Maybe I can write about that gorgeous purple sweater I just bought."

"And we don't have to write exclusively about sixth-grade news the way that drippy *Sixers* does," Lila added. "We can have seventh- and eighth-grade news, too. The whole middle school will want to read our paper."

"That's a terrific idea, Lila," Janet said. "I'll write the eighth-grade column." She paused and reconsidered. "No, I can't do that. I'll be writing the editorial column." She looked around the table. "After all, I *am* the president of the Unicorns," she said. "The club president should be the editor of the Unicorn newspaper, don't you think?"

Jessica frowned down at the table. The newspaper had been *her* brilliant idea, and she'd been hoping that everybody would agree that she should be the editor. That would really show Elizabeth.

But Janet seemed to think the job was already hers, and nobody wanted to argue with her. Janet was not very nice to people who didn't see things her way.

"We'll have a meeting this afternoon at my house," Janet told them, "to plan the first issue." She gave Jessica a warm smile. "We already have one article—Jessica's. I think it should be on the front page. Along with the editorial column, of course."

"Sounds great, Janet," Jessica said trying to force a smile. Clearly, Janet was not willing to consider letting another Unicorn be in charge of the newspaper.

Janet picked up her milk carton. "Now, I think we ought to have a toast. To Jessica, for her fabulous newspaper idea. Thank you, Jessica."

All the Unicorns raised their milk cartons. "To Jessica!" they echoed.

This time Jessica's smile was sincere.

"I still don't think they'll do it," Amy said, as she and Elizabeth walked toward the bike rack that afternoon after school. "You know the Unicorns. The minute they have to work hard, they run in the opposite direction." She giggled. "Except for Mary Wallace, not one of them even knows how to type, let alone write an article!"

"I hope you're right, Amy," Elizabeth said quietly. All day she had been hearing the rumors that the Unicorns were going to start a newspaper of their own to compete with the *Sixers*, and she was beginning to get a little worried. Amy's attempts to cheer her up were not helping very much.

Elizabeth unlocked her bike. "Oh, there's Jess," she said, looking up, "and she's by herself. Would you mind if I spoke to her alone?"

"I'll wait for you at the corner," Amy said.

Elizabeth wheeled her bike over to where Jessica was standing. All day she had been thinking about what she should say. Jessica had been so angry that morning she wouldn't listen to any explanation, no matter how reasonable. Elizabeth hoped that by now Jessica might have cooled down enough to discuss what had happened.

"Hi, Jess," Elizabeth said. She hesitated. "I—I just wanted to say that I'm sorry about—"

"Oh, don't be sorry," Jessica said.

Elizabeth felt instantly relieved. "Then you're not angry any more?"

There was a gleam in Jessica's eye. "Actually," she said, "I'm glad things happened the way they did."

Elizabeth raised her eyebrows. "You're glad?" she asked uncertainly.

"Of *course* I'm glad," Jessica retorted. "Why shouldn't I be? Things are turning out just perfectly. My unimportant story, the one *you* didn't want, is going to appear in the first issue of the Unicorn newspaper." She gave Elizabeth an I-told-you-so smile. "On the front page!"

Elizabeth bit her lip. So the Unicorns were still planning to go ahead with the newspaper.

"Jessica," she said in a low voice, "putting out a newspaper takes a lot of work. Besides, there's probably not room for *two* newspapers at this school."

Jessica gave a short laugh. "That's really what you're afraid of, isn't it, Elizabeth? You're afraid our newspaper will be so good that nobody will want to read yours."

"No, I'm not," Elizabeth replied, starting to get angry all over again. "I just don't want you to do all this work just to make *me* mad!"

"Oh, Elizabeth, don't worry about us!" She turned away from Elizabeth and waved at Lila and Ellen. "Now, if you'll excuse me, I've got to go. We're having a meeting this afternoon to organize our first issue, and I don't want to be late." She started to go, then turned back. "Oh, and thank you for rejecting my article," she said in an angry voice. "If it hadn't been for you, I might never have gotten my brilliant idea!"

Elizabeth watched as Jessica walked away with her friends. *If that's the way you feel, Jessica,* she said to herself, *then the battle of the newspapers is on!*

"As your editor," Janet instructed, "I have put together a list of things that we have to discuss. Number one, the name for our newspaper. How does everyone like The *Unicorn News*?"

"Or how about *Unicorn Tales*?" Tamara Chase suggested.

"*I* think we ought to call it *Hoof Print*," Lila said. She looked around as if she were expecting something from them. "Get it?" she asked. "Hoof *Print*."

"Oh, that's funny, Lila," Mary said with a laugh.

"How about the *Purple Post*?" Jessica suggested.

For the next ten minutes, they discussed names. They had lots of suggestions; everyone had at least one. But when they took a vote, they couldn't agree on which one was best.

"Well, we don't have to pick a name right now," Janet said irritably. She was obviously upset that almost nobody liked her name, The *Unicorn News*. "The second thing we have to decide is who our editors will be." She looked around. "As you all know, I will be editor-in-chief. We still need a number of other editors to be in charge of various departments. These editors will report back to me. Just like the committee heads for the dance," she concluded.

Suddenly, everyone was talking at once. Everybody wanted to be an editor, but they couldn't agree on who would do which job. Everybody agreed, though, that Mary Wallace should be the production manager, since she was the only one who could type. Finally Janet held up her hand.

"We'll have to hold an election," she said. "Or maybe I should just assign people. Anyway, we can put that off until next time." She looked down at her list. "The third thing to decide is the layout of the newspaper itself. The number of pages we're going to print and the kinds of articles we ought to have are two examples."

"I think we ought to print it on purple paper," Lila said. "That way, everybody would know right away that it's the Unicorn paper."

Everybody looked at her admiringly. "What a good idea," Ellen said.

"But won't the purple paper make it awfully hard to read?" Mary Wallace asked. There was a silence while everybody thought about that.

"Maybe *light* purple paper would do," Ellen offered.

"OK, that's decided. Now, what about the articles?" Janet asked. "Let's list the kinds we're looking for."

By the time everybody had made their suggestions, Mary had filled up a whole page writing down their ideas.

"This list is much too long," Janet said authoritatively. "The editors can come up with a shorter one." Since there were no editors, it was not clear just when there would be a shorter list. Nobody seemed to mind.

The rest of the meeting was more of the same.

The Unicorns could not agree on anything. Finally, after an hour's discussion, Janet summed up what they had decided.

"We'll print our newspaper on light purple paper," she announced. "And we'll postpone the other decisions." She smiled a satisfied smile. "Now, let's hear the reports from the dance committees."

"I'll report on the music," Lila volunteered. "My committee has decided that people are sick of the same old thing. The trouble is, we don't have enough money to hire an out-of-town band to play for the entire evening."

"We know that already, Lila," Janet said impatiently. "What we need to know is how to solve this problem."

"I was just getting to that part," Lila said confidently. "As you know, my uncle works for a record company in Los Angeles. He's sure to know a band that would be glad to do a few numbers at the end of the dance, just for the publicity. So, we can have a local band and advertise a special mystery guest."

"Very good, Lila," Janet said approvingly.

"And we can run a story about the mystery guest in our newspaper," Jessica said, thinking out loud. "That's sure to help sell tickets."

"*Very* good, Jessica," Janet said, sounding especially pleased at the mention of increased ticket sales. She looked thoughtful. "You know, I'm considering making you our news editor."

Jessica leaned back, feeling very happy. News editor! Things were working out perfectly.

Four

◇

"Have you heard the latest news?" Amy asked Elizabeth the next morning in homeroom.

Elizabeth managed a small smile. "If you're talking about the Unicorns' newspaper, I know everything there is to know. Jess told me."

The night before, as the twins did the dishes, Jessica had been bubbling over with excitement about the possibility of being elected news editor. She had been full of ideas, most of which were pretty unrealistic. Elizabeth knew Jessica was trying to make her feel bad, so she had tried to pretend that nothing Jessica was saying bothered her.

But the truth was that Elizabeth felt miserable. The Unicorn newspaper only existed because

Jessica wanted to get back at her, and that hurt a lot. But she could not tell Jessica how upset she was. If she did, Jessica would only accuse her of being afraid that the *Sixers* couldn't stand up against competition.

"Julie told me," Amy went on, "that Lila wanted to call it *Hoof Print.*" She giggled. "Isn't that ridiculous?"

"Would you mind," Elizabeth asked quietly, "if we changed the subject? I'm kind of tired of hearing about the Unicorn newspaper."

"Sure," Amy replied sympathetically. "Did you hear about Lois Waller?"

"Lois? What about Lois?" Elizabeth asked. Lots of the other kids teased Lois about being overweight, but Elizabeth liked her. She admired Lois's sense of determination. If Lois decided to do something, she really worked at it.

"Well, nothing new really. It's just that Bruce Patman was teasing her again," Amy reported. "He offered a dollar to anyone who could guess how much she weighs."

Elizabeth frowned. "Poor Lois," she said. "I wish everyone would give her a chance. She really has a lot of good qualities."

"She's a great cartoonist," Amy agreed.

"I've got an idea," Elizabeth exclaimed. "Let's

ask her if she'll do another drawing for the *Sixers*. Everybody liked the last one she did."

Amy nodded approvingly. "That's a good idea, Elizabeth. She'll like that."

Elizabeth, thinking of ways to make Lois Waller feel better, was beginning to feel a little better herself. "You know what, Amy?" she said. "I'm going to make the next edition of the *Sixers* the best ever. Unicorns or no Unicorns!"

That afternoon, there was another Unicorn meeting.

"This time," Janet said, "we really *must* get organized. I've made a list of the editors I want. I'll read your names."

Jessica squirmed. If there was an election, she thought she had a chance of being chosen news editor. But with Janet making all the decisions she could not be sure.

"I thought," Lila objected tactfully, "that we were going to have an election."

"Elections take too long," Janet replied. "So here's the list. Ellen, you'll be our fashion editor."

"Terrific!" Ellen shrieked. "I can write all about Unicorn style."

Janet continued reading. "Lila, you'll be entertainment editor. That's because your uncle works at a record company and you get all the latest news about the entertainment world."

Lila looked pleased.

"Mary, of course, will be the production manager." Janet named several others, until everybody had a job. Everybody, that is, except for Jessica. Jessica could hardly stand the suspense. Finally, Janet looked up from her list. "I've been saving the most important position for last," she said. "The news editor is second in command to the editor-in-chief. Jessica, I'm appointing you news editor."

Jessica looked around with an elated smile. News editor. Second in command to the editor-in-chief. It sounded absolutely wonderful!

"Now," Janet said, "we'll print the paper once a week. It will have eight pages. That'll give us space to print some really important things. Like the history of the Unicorns, for example. Tamara, you can write that."

"Eight pages?" Ellen asked. "Isn't that a lot? The *Sixers* is only half that long."

Mary looked a bit worried. "I hope I won't have to do *all* the typing. Eight dittos per week is a big job."

"Oh, no," Janet assured her breezily. "We'll help."

"But no one types except me," Mary pointed out.

"Then I'll get my father's secretary to do it," Janet said casually. "Don't worry."

There was a gleam in Lila's eye. "The *Sixers* comes out on Wednesdays," she said. "I think we should put our paper out on Tuesdays."

"On Tuesday?" Ellen asked. "Today is Thursday!"

Lila laughed. "I know, but this way, we'll beat out the *Sixers*. We'll print the news before they do. Nobody will bother reading that wimpy little paper after they've read ours!"

The Unicorns cheered. Jessica cheered too, even though she felt a tiny bit sorry for Elizabeth.

"And one last thing," Janet said, clearing her throat. "I've decided on a name. We'll call it The *Unicorn News*."

There was silence. Several people looked as though they wanted to disagree, but nobody had the nerve to speak up. Jessica thought it was a boring name, but she wasn't about to say so. As second-in-command, it was her duty to be loyal.

"I think it's a great name for a *fabulous* newspaper," Jessica said finally.

Janet smiled. "Good," she said heartily. "Now all you editors can get to work."

*   *   *

As news editor, Jessica completely devoted herself to the first issue of The *Unicorn News*. She made a list of the news articles that needed to be written for the first issue. Then she put down the names of people who could write the articles. Then she got the writers to agree, which turned out to be the hardest job of all. Most of the writers complained that they already had too much to do. They couldn't *possibly* write their articles overnight!

But Jessica was firm. "I must have your articles by tomorrow," she insisted. "That'll give Mary and Mr. Howell's secretary the whole weekend to type them up, and we can run the paper off on Monday."

In the meantime, Lila bought the paper supply. All of the Unicorns were very unhappy to learn that the paper would cost almost fifteen dollars. That was nearly one third of what they had in the Unicorn treasury. Still, Lila was very pleased with her purchase. The paper was a vibrant purple. She knew she was supposed to buy light purple, but when she saw the deep purple paper in the store, she could not resist.

On Friday, Janet stopped Jessica in the hallway between classes and handed her a piece of paper. "Here's Ellen's fashion article," she said hurriedly and turned to go.

Jessica looked at the story. The headline read, PURPLE IS THIS SEASON'S FASHION COLOR, and it was about Ellen's new sweater. Three words in the first sentence were misspelled.

"What am I supposed to do with this?" Jessica asked.

Janet looked surprised. "Well," she replied, "you might start by correcting the spelling."

"But I'm the *news* editor," Jessica protested. "This is a *fashion* article. I've already got to edit all the news articles I've assigned."

"Well, you don't expect *me* to do it, do you?" Janet replied. "I'm busy planning the dance, you know. Don't forget—you're second-in-command." Janet began to leaf through her notebook. "I just remembered," she said. "Lila gave me her entertainment article. You'd better have a look at that, too. And Kimberly handed in some Unicorn party recipes. Some of the quantities don't look right, but I'm sure you can fix them."

Jessica sighed. She knew better than to argue with Janet. But she wasn't sure how she was going to get everything done. The time was passing awfully fast.

By Friday afternoon, things had gone from

bad to worse for Jessica. As the editors turned in
their work, Janet gave the articles to Jessica for editing. Most of the stories were very badly written,
and Jessica had to spend hours trying to get them
in shape. Even worse, the stories were all much
shorter than Jessica had expected. Tamara was
supposed to write two pages on the history of the
Unicorns, but her article was merely two paragraphs long. Ellen's fashion story was one para-
graph. Lila's review of Donny Diamond's latest
album was just three paragraphs. And when Jessica asked her friends for the news articles she had
assigned, she found that only one person had
bothered to write anything at all!

"It's *terrible*," Jessica moaned at three-thirty
on Friday afternoon. Jessica, Mary, Lila, and Ellen
were having ice cream at Casey's Ice Cream Parlor
in the Valley Mall. "I'll bet we don't have enough
stuff to fill up even four pages. How will we ever
fill up eight?"

"Don't tell me your problems," Mary said
grimly. "Janet forgot to check with her father's secretary about typing the dittos for us. She's on vacation, and I have to type the whole thing!"

"Oh, no," Jessica said sympathetically. She
sighed. Hundreds of times that week, she had
dreamed of giving up. But then she would imag-

ine Elizabeth giving her an I-told-you-so look, and she would turn back to her duties with new energy. *I'll show you, Elizabeth*, she told herself now, *I'll get my "unimportant" story in print even if it kills me!* "Don't worry, Mary," she said. "I'll help you. I can't type, but I can help decide where to put things."

"I'd help, too," Lila said, "but I'm going to Los Angeles with my father. We have tickets to a show."

"I'd help, too," Ellen said, "but I promised Tamara that I'd go shopping with her."

Mary looked alarmed. "You mean Jessica and I have to put the newspaper together all by ourselves?"

"Oh, there's nothing to it," Lila said in a comforting voice. "Anyway, we'll run the ditto machine on Monday."

Jessica and Mary exchanged glances. It was going to be a long weekend.

The next morning, Jessica went over to Mary's house and they started to work. As soon as they put all the stories together, they could see that there wasn't nearly enough material to fill eight pages. They put Jessica's article, Janet's editorial, and Tamara's history of the Unicorns on the front page. On the second page, they put Lila's review

and the one news story that Jessica had been able
to come up with, which was about the dance.
Kimberly's recipes and Ellen's fashion article took
up all of page three.

And that was it.

"What are we going to do?" Mary wailed.
"We don't have enough to fill up the paper!"

"Sure we do," Jessica said, trying to sound
confident. After all, she *was* second-in-command.
She couldn't let Mary see how worried she was.
"We can print the minutes from one of our meetings."

"But do you think anybody will be interested
in reading that?" Mary asked slowly.

"Oh, I'm sure they will," Jessica replied, feeling more sure of herself. "After all, people are
always asking us what goes on at our meetings.
Now they can see for themselves. And we've got a
copy of the letter that Lila and Ellen wrote to the
TV station to complain that the station wasn't re-
porting enough on Donny Diamond."

"Maybe we should have only six pages,"
Mary suggested, sounding a little more hopeful.

"I think that would be a good idea," Jessica
agreed. "Do you think you can type all this today?"

Mary surveyed the work. "I guess," she said

doubtfully. "But I wish Janet had remembered to ask her father's secretary for help."

"It probably wouldn't have done any good," Jessica said. "I doubt that secretaries work on weekends."

"You mean I have to type this newspaper *every* weekend?" Mary asked indignantly.

Jessica was speechless. She had entirely forgotten that this was only the first edition of The *Unicorn News*.

"I'm sorry, girls," Mrs. Knight, the principal's secretary, said, "but I can't let you use the ditto machine today."

"But our paper's supposed to come out tomorrow!" Jessica exclaimed.

It was Monday, and Jessica had run into yet another snag. When Jessica, Mary, Lila, and Ellen had showed up in the principal's office with their dittos, they found out that Mrs. Knight was running off a big project.

"It can go out on Wednesday, can't it?" the secretary asked. "That's the day the sixth-grade paper comes out."

Lila stuck out her lip when she heard that. But they didn't have any choice.

So at lunchtime on Tuesday, they took the dittos to the office again. This time, Mr. Bowman met them at the door. "I'm sorry," he said politely, "but the ditto machine is assigned to the *Sixers* during Tuesday lunch period."

"But we were hoping to get our paper out tomorrow," Jessica said.

"Well, maybe you can come back this afternoon after school," Mr. Bowman suggested helpfully. "I don't think the machine is scheduled to be in use then."

"I can't come," Mary said. "I'm going to the dentist."

"Ellen and Jessica and I can't come either," Lila said. "The dance committee is having a mandatory meeting."

"How about lunch period tomorrow?" Mr. Bowman offered.

"I guess that's the only thing we can do," Jessica replied, shaking her head.

"Uh, Jessica," Lila said carefully, "don't forget that the Boosters are meeting at lunch tomorrow. But it wouldn't hurt if you missed a meeting," she added quickly. "Why don't you and Mary make the dittos tomorrow?"

Jessica gave Lila a nasty look. "Things had better improve for the next issue," she warned. "Mary and I can't keep doing this all by ourselves."

"Oh, we'll help next time," Ellen promised.

"And we'll make sure the others do, too," Lila agreed.

"I *hope* so," Jessica said.

So, on Wednesday, Jessica and Mary went to the principal's office to run off copies of the first *Unicorn News*. Every so often Jessica would look up from her work and stare moodily out of the office door, watching the other students pass by and wishing she were out there with her friends. Mary didn't look much happier than Jessica felt.

They were almost finished making the copies when Mrs. Knight interrupted them. "Girls," she said, "have you noticed that your newspaper is, uh, a little difficult to read?" For the first time, Jessica took a good look at the copies they had made, and she realized that Mrs. Knight was just being polite. The deep purple paper Lila had bought was almost the same shade as the ink from the ditto machine. The newspaper was close to *impossible* to read. But the process had taken nearly the entire lunch hour, and Jessica refused to consider doing it over again.

On Thursday morning, Lila and Ellen and Kimberly Haver helped Jessica and Mary take the paper to all the homerooms.

"I can't wait to hear what people say," Ellen exclaimed happily as they distributed the last bunch of papers.

"Neither can I," Lila said. "I just hope we ran off enough copies."

We? Yeah, right, Jessica thought. She and Mary had done all the work. Lila was no help at all. Jessica looked at the stacks of papers. She knew there was room for improvement, but she couldn't help feeling proud. Everyone would want to read the first edition of The *Unicorn News*. Maybe they'd even have to run off more copies!

But at noon, when Jessica checked the homerooms to see whether there were any papers left, she couldn't believe what she saw. Only a few papers had been taken, probably by the Unicorns themselves.

She had to admit it: The first edition of *The Unicorn News* was an embarrassing failure.

Five

◇

"I guess we don't have to worry about the competition, after all," Amy said with a good-natured laugh.

The *Sixers* was having a staff meeting. Several of them had brought copies of the first edition of The *Unicorn News*, and everybody was talking about it.

"The problem is that you can't read it," Sophia Rizzo pointed out. "Using purple paper was a big mistake."

Amy was flipping through the paper and squinting at it. "But when you take the trouble to read it, it's a *scream*. Get this—the minutes of one of their meetings!"

"Oh, terrific," Julie Porter said. "I've always wondered what they do at their meetings."

"Well, you don't have to wonder any longer," Amy replied. "At this meeting, they spent ten minutes trying to decide what their least favorite color is. Anybody want to guess what they decided?"

"Yellow?" Sophia suggested.

"Why should anybody spend ten minutes talking about *that*?" Julie wanted to know.

"Who knows why the Unicorns do anything?" Amy asked. "Anyway, it was green. Purple, of course, is their favorite. I guess that's why they like grape sherbet. There's a recipe for it on page three." She peered at the recipe. "According to this, sherbet takes four *gallons* of grape juice. That's a lot of grape juice!"

Julie and Amy broke into a fit of giggles.

"It must be a misprint," Elizabeth said seriously. She had the suspicion that most of the work that had gone into the Unicorn paper had been Jessica's. For her sister's sake, she was sorry that the paper was such a miserable flop. Jessica must be terribly embarrassed. But maybe it was just as well. Her twin needed to learn just how much effort went into a newspaper. Maybe then she'd appreciate the *Sixers* a little more.

"I just don't understand it," Janet said. "Why *didn't* people read The *News*?"

"Because," Lila said in a self-satisfied tone of voice, "the paper was late. We should have gotten it out on Tuesday, the way I suggested. People just didn't want to read another paper after they'd read the *Sixers*."

"I think it was because the paper we printed it on was too dark," Kimberly said. "You couldn't read it at *all*."

Janet scowled. "Well," she said, "if we can't do it right, maybe we shouldn't do it at all."

"I agree," Tamara said quickly. "If people don't want to read about the Unicorns, we won't try to force them. It's their loss."

"Anyway," Mary said, "it was too much work. I vote we give it up."

"But that would be admitting defeat!" Jessica exclaimed. "We can't let Elizabeth—I mean, we can't let everyone—think the Unicorns just gave up!"

Janet looked uncertain. "Jessica's right," she said slowly. "We've got our reputation to think of."

"And anyway," Jessica added, seeing that Janet was hesitating, "I still believe in The *Unicorn News*, even if we did make a few mistakes. We know we can't depend on the *Sixers*. We need to have our own paper so we can print the things *we* want to print!"

"I do want to do another story about the dance," Janet admitted. She nodded, suddenly decisive. "All right, we'll print another issue. But this time, Jessica, you're the one who's responsible. I'm too busy with the dance to be bothered editing articles and correcting misspelled words. I'm appointing you editor-in-chief."

Jessica nodded calmly, but inside she was elated. Editor-in-chief! That would show Elizabeth!

Mary sighed. "Well, I guess if we're going to give it another shot, I'm willing to help."

"I'll help, too," Ellen volunteered eagerly. "I'll write another fashion article." She paused thoughtfully. "I'll call it WHAT THE UNICORNS ARE WEARING THIS SPRING."

Jessica smiled at her editors. *All of them*, she thought triumphantly, *report to me now!* "Why don't we hold an editorial meeting at my house tomorrow?" she said.

An editorial meeting. All the way home, Jessica said the words over again to herself, loving the way they sounded. An editorial meeting, chaired by Jessica Wakefield, editor-in-chief!

"So Janet appointed *me* editor-in-chief," Jessica proudly told her family that night at dinner.

She sneaked a glance at Elizabeth to see how she was taking the news. The twins had barely spoken for a week. "We're going to have the best newspaper in the world," she bragged. "The *very* best!" Jessica wanted to make the most of her moment of triumph.

Elizabeth stared down at her plate. The Unicorns' first effort had been a disaster. Didn't Jessica realize that the few people who bothered to read it were laughing about it? She thought the Unicorns should give up the idea of a paper, but she knew there was no point in telling her twin that.

"Editor-in-chief, huh?" asked the twins' fourteen-year-old brother, Steven. "I guess we'll have to call you Big Chief Jessie." He put his hand to his mouth and did an Indian war-whoop. "Woo-woo-woo-woo."

"Oh, you are just *so* funny, Steven," Jessica said sarcastically. "It's an amazing privilege to eat dinner with the funniest boy in Sweet Valley." She glanced at Elizabeth. "Isn't it, Elizabeth?" she asked sweetly.

Elizabeth didn't answer.

"Why, of course it is, Your Chiefship," Steven replied. "An unbelievable privilege."

"Steven," Mrs. Wakefield said, "please take

your elbows off the table." She smiled at Jessica. "Congratulations, Jessica." Gently, she put her hand on Elizabeth's arm. "Isn't it wonderful that your sister's been named editor, Elizabeth? Now there are *two* editors in the Wakefield family."

Jessica beamed. But Elizabeth just sat stiff and unsmiling. She hated to feud with her sister, especially in front of her parents. But she didn't want to congratulate Jessica, not after the way she'd acted. Still, her mother was waiting. "Congratulations, Jessica," Elizabeth finally managed to say. "And good luck!" she added.

The next afternoon, the Unicorn editors met in the Wakefields' den. Before Jessica called the meeting to order, she stood in front of the room and looked over the notes she had made. She had spent the entire evening before studying old copies of the *Sixers* in order to get some ideas for *her* paper. Of course she would not tell Elizabeth, but she admired the good work the *Sixers* staff did. Now that she understood the problems involved in putting out a newspaper, it was a little easier to appreciate Elizabeth's work.

Jessica looked around. Everybody was there but Tamara. They'd better get started. She clapped her hands. The Unicorns stopped chattering among themselves and looked at her expectantly.

"I hope that we're going to do things differently this time," Mary Wallace said. She made a face. "I don't want to be typing all day Saturday and Sunday."

Jessica gave everyone a firm look. "Things are going to be *very* different," she said. "We'll start by changing the name."

"You mean, we're going to call it *Hoof Prints* after all?" Lila asked hopefully.

Jessica shook her head. "No. We're going to call it The *Middle School News*. That way, it will attract more students. People probably didn't read it last time because they thought it was news *for* the Unicorns."

"The *Middle School News*," Kimberly said. "That sounds very professional."

"We'll print it on white paper," Jessica went on. "And we'll keep it down to four pages."

"Oh, good," Mary said, relieved. "I can easily manage four pages in a weekend."

"And most of our articles," Jessica went on, "not *all*, but most, will be articles about what's happening at school. People don't want to read a whole newspaper full of stuff about the Unicorns." She blushed a little, remembering a remark she had overheard in the hall. Two seventh-grade girls

Jessica didn't know had been laughing and saying that it was silly to waste time arguing over your least favorite color. She was almost glad that so few people had read the first edition.

"But if we do all that, our paper will be just like the *Sixers*," Ellen complained.

"No, it won't," Jessica countered forcefully. "Our articles will be *exciting*. We won't have dumb stuff like student council interviews, or articles on Coach Cassel's broken leg." She shook her head. "The *Sixers* is awfully *boring*."

"So what will we write about?" Kimberly wanted to know. "What kind of stories did you have in mind?"

"Well, we'll have class news, of course," Jessica said. "And then we'll—we'll—" She paused, at a loss. "I don't want to do *all* the planning," she said. "You guys are the editors. What kind of exciting articles would *you* like to do?"

But nobody could come up with anything more exciting than the articles that the *Sixers* usually ran. In fact, everything they thought of had already been done in the *Sixers* at least once.

Jessica was beginning to feel a little uneasy. They had to come up with *something* interesting, or their second paper would be as big a flop as their first.

Just at that moment, Tamara Chase dashed in. She was out of breath.

"I'm sorry I'm late," she apologized. "But as I was coming out of school, I saw somebody who looked exactly like Donny Diamond! I followed him all the way across town. I was hoping to get his autograph."

"Oh, wow," Kimberly breathed. "You actually saw Donny Diamond—in person?" She gave Tamara an admiring look, as if some of Donny Diamond might have rubbed off on her.

"Did you get his autograph?" Ellen demanded excitedly, jumping up from her seat. "Let me see."

"It turned out it wasn't him," Tamara explained, and all the Unicorns let out a collective groan of disappointment.

"Hey, Tamara," Ellen said, "you followed some guy all the way across town for nothing."

Lila leaned forward. "It wasn't for nothing," she said. Her eyes were sparkling. "It's given me a wonderful idea for the newspaper."

Tamara looked puzzled. "The newspaper?"

"We've been trying to come up with exciting ideas for articles," Ellen explained to her. "But we haven't thought of anything."

"*I* have," Lila said. "What do you think about featuring an interview with Donny Diamond?"

"An interview?" Ellen screamed. "Lila, that's a *perfect* idea!"

"It would be a perfect idea," Mary said, "if there was any way we could *get* an interview with Donny Diamond."

"That's right, Lila," Jessica interjected, trying to regain control of the meeting. "We don't know Donny Diamond. How are we supposed to get an interview with him?"

"That's easy," Lila said enthusiastically. "We don't really have to interview him! We know everything there is to know about Donny Diamond, don't we? We don't have to ask him any questions, we already know the answers!"

"You're right, Lila," Ellen said. "We can make up the answers just as well as the questions."

"Hey, wait a minute," Jessica objected. "Won't people be curious about how we got to know Donny Diamond? Won't they figure out what we're doing?" The one thing they *didn't* need was another big embarrassment.

"Not if we tell them that my uncle introduced us to him," Lila said triumphantly. "After all, don't forget that he works for a big record company. We can say that he gave us Donny's home number and Donny invited us to interview him. Nobody will guess the truth."

Jessica hesitated. What Lila was suggesting

wasn't exactly honest. But then Jessica thought about how everyone would react to reading an interview with Donny Diamond in their very own *Middle School News*. Everyone would want a copy to read and keep for a souvenir! Their paper, *her* paper, would be an instant success!

"You know, Lila," she said thoughtfully, "I think you've got a good idea."

Lila looked delighted. "Thank you," she said.

"Then we're agreed," Jessica said, already beginning to feel excited. "In our next issue, we'll feature an interview with Donny Diamond!"

Just let Elizabeth and the *Sixers* try to top *that*!

Six

◇

"We know the date of Donny's birthday and where he was born and all that," Jessica said, making notes. "So we can put that stuff at the beginning of the article." She looked around. "Now, who's got a question?"

It was Saturday morning, and all of the Unicorn editors were at Lila's house working on the feature interview for The *Middle School News*.

"Here's a good one," Ellen replied. "What's your favorite animal, Donny?"

"That's easy," several Unicorns squealed. "It's a unicorn, of course!"

"What's your favorite color, Donny?" Kimberly asked.

"Purple!" they all chorused gleefully.

"And your favorite dessert?"

"Grape sherbet!"

"Don't you think these questions are kind of silly?" Mary asked with a doubtful look. "I mean, people will want some *real* information."

"I agree with Mary," Jessica said seriously. "We have to give our readers more than grape sherbet."

But they had run out of questions. Nobody could come up with anything interesting.

"I know!" Lila said at last, snapping her fingers. "There was an interview with Donny in *SMASH!* a couple of months ago. We can take some stuff from that. I'll go upstairs and get it."

With the help of the *SMASH!* article, they came up with some really good questions, such as "Where did you get your start in music?" and "Which of your albums is your favorite?" They were careful not to copy anything from the article word for word, but it helped them to see what a real interview was like.

At the end of an hour, Jessica sat back, feeling very satisfied. "I think we've got enough stuff here for a *really* exciting interview," she said. "I wish we could print a picture of Donny. But that would be impossible unless we photocopied the paper instead of running it off on the ditto machine."

"Wouldn't that cost a lot?" Mary asked.

"Maybe we could *sell* the paper," Kimberly suggested. "We could charge enough to cover the cost of the copying, and maybe have a little left over for the treasury."

"That's a great idea," Jessica said enthusiastically. "The treasury could really use some extra money. Especially after we spent so much on purple paper." Then she stopped, remembering last week's giant flop, and how they had been left with stacks and stacks of newspapers that they had to throw away. "But maybe we'd better go slow at first. Let's not charge until we know whether or not anyone is going to read our paper."

Lila's eyes were sparkling. "I've got something that's just as good as a picture," she said. "And we can run it off on the ditto without any problem."

"What is it?" Jessica asked curiously.

Lila smiled. "Donny's autograph!"

"Donny Diamond's autograph?" Ellen asked. "When did you get *that*?"

"Remember that letter I got from the Donny Diamond Fan Club last month?" Lila told her.

"Well, his signature was stamped at the bottom. All we have to do is trace it. It'll look just like he personally signed the interview. Nobody will know the difference."

"That's a fabulous idea!" Ellen said.

Mary shook her head. "But isn't it called forgery when you trace somebody's signature? Couldn't we get in trouble for copying?"

"Oh, don't be such a worrywart, Mary," Lila scoffed. "The signature was in a letter that the fan club sent me. I can do anything I want with my letter, can't I?"

"I guess so," Mary agreed. "But we still have to worry about finishing the other articles we want for this week's edition. We don't have much time."

"The next step, after we collect all of our articles," Jessica said, "is for Mary to type the dittos. I don't think we can get this issue out on Tuesday, but we can certainly make it by Wednesday, the same day the *Sixers* comes out. Who'll volunteer to help me run the pages off on Tuesday after school?" Excited by Jessica's enthusiasm, everybody raised their hands.

First thing on Monday morning, Jessica got permission from Mrs. Knight to use the ditto machine the next day after school. So on Tuesday afternoon, the Unicorns met in the school principal's office to run off their newspaper. And on Wednesday morning, right on schedule, Jessica, Lila, and Ellen delivered the papers to all the homerooms in the middle school. In the sixth-grade homerooms, they stacked their newspapers beside the copies of the *Sixers* that were already there.

Jessica was putting the papers in Mr. Davis's homeroom when Caroline Pearce came hurrying up and grabbed a copy right out of her hands.

"I heard your paper is running an interview with Donny Diamond," she panted breathlessly. "I hope it's true. I've been telling *everybody* about it, and they're all planning to get copies. Even my older sister Anita wants one."

"It's true, all right," Jessica assured Caroline, handing her another copy for her sister. "I hope you enjoy it."

"Oh, I *will*," Caroline said, clutching her papers and sighing dramatically. "Donny Diamond is *so* fabulous!"

Jessica surpressed a giggle. Caroline wrote the gossip column for the *Sixers*. She certainly wasn't being very loyal—she hadn't even bothered to pick up a copy of the *Sixers*!

But Jessica didn't have time to think about

Caroline, because she was practically mobbed an instant later. All the sixth-graders wanted a copy of Jessica's paper, and the entire stack vanished before the first bell rang. The latecomers were terribly disappointed when they discovered that the papers were gone.

Jessica did have time to notice that everybody was so excited about the interview in The *News*, hardly anyone picked up a copy of the *Sixers*. It was no wonder, she thought. The *Sixers* was featuring profiles of the cafeteria staff—not exactly thrilling material.

It was the same all over school. By lunchtime, there were no more copies of The *Middle School News* left, and Jessica and several of the Unicorns had to spend the lunch hour running off extra copies.

"We'll probably need sixty more copies," Jessica said to Mary. She switched on the ditto machine. "I hope the dittos are still OK."

Tamara Chase came hurrying in. "We can use about twenty more copies in the seventh-grade homerooms," she said. "And Janet says they need fifteen more copies for the eighth grade."

Jessica did some quick addition. "Make that a total of ninety-five more copies," she told Mary.

"It's just wonderful," Lila said. "Everybody's talking about Donny Diamond and the Unicorns."

"It sounds like a great new rock group," Ellen said, giggling.

Jessica closed her eyes blissfully. "Donny Diamond and the Unicorns," she said, thinking about the piles and piles of newspapers people had snatched up that morning. "What a perfect combination!"

"I can't believe it," Elizabeth said, shaking her head. "Almost nobody took a copy of our paper."

Elizabeth and the *Sixers* staff were eating lunch together in the cafeteria. They were bewildered. For the first time since they had started publishing the *Sixers*, several copies of the paper were left over. Most of them, in fact.

Sophia Rizzo opened her milk carton. "That's because everybody's too busy reading the Unicorn paper to read ours. Who wants to read an interview with the head cafeteria cook when they can read an interview with Donny Diamond?"

"Sophia's right," Julie Porter said, wrinkling up her nose in disgust. "Everybody's talking about Donny Diamond and the Unicorns."

"Sounds stupid to me," Amy Sutton grumbled. She took a bite out of her sandwich. "What I want to know," she added suspiciously, "is how in the world they got that interview. And the autograph, too. Lots of people are taking copies of the paper just so they can have Donny Diamond's autograph."

Elizabeth sighed. "Caroline Pearce told me that Lila's uncle is in the music business," she said. "She says that's how they got Donny Diamond's phone number and the interview." She shook her head, looking puzzled. "It's funny that Jessica hasn't mentioned anything at home about interviewing Donny Diamond. Of course," Elizabeth admitted slowly, "Jessica and I haven't said much to each other in quite a while."

"Do you think there's something fishy going on?" Amy asked, narrowing her eyes.

Elizabeth shrugged. "It doesn't make any difference," she said. "The thing I'm worried about most is competing with them. Obviously, we're going to have to come up with something pretty interesting, or it'll be the same thing all over again next week."

"Especially if they run another interview," Sophia said.

"We're scheduled to print the story about the new science books," Elizabeth reminded them.

Amy made a face. "Not a very exciting subject, if you ask me. About on the same level as interviews with the cafeteria staff."

"Maybe the interviews aren't very entertaining," Elizabeth admitted, "but they're necessary. People ought to know what's happening at school."

Sophia laughed sadly. "That might be. But I'm afraid that interviews with cafeteria cooks just can't measure up to an interview with a rock star."

"I wonder," Amy said thoughtfully, "what the Unicorns will manage to come up with next."

At that instant, Nora Mercandy walked up with her tray. "Hi," she said. "Have you seen the posters?"

"Posters?" Elizabeth asked curiously. "What posters?"

"The posters advertising next week's *News*," Nora told them. "Lila and Ellen are putting them up."

"What do they say?" Amy asked.

Nora looked grim. "They say, 'Send in your questions for Donny Diamond now! Answers published in next week's *Middle School News*. On sale next Tuesday. Only fifteen cents.'"

"I can't believe it," Amy breathed, her eyes widening. "They've done it again!"

Elizabeth couldn't believe it either. This time Jessica and the Unicorns had the nerve to charge money for their paper!

Seven

◇

"Isn't this wonderful?" Jessica asked, happily sifting through the dozens of 'Dear Donny' letters the Unicorns had received. There were so many questions to answer that it looked as if there would be no room in the *News* for news—except about the big dance, of course. But that was fine as far as Jessica was concerned. The fewer news stories they printed, the easier her job as editor-in-chief would be.

"I can't believe so many people want Donny Diamond to answer their questions!" Jessica added.

"You'd better believe it," Mary said, opening another envelope, "because we have to come up with the answers." She unfolded a piece of notebook paper and broke into a grin as she read it. "Listen to this," she said. "'Dear Donny, I've been dying to know something *really* personal about you,'" Mary paused dramatically. "'Where was your favorite vacation?'" Mary giggled. "That doesn't sound very *personal* to me."

Lila waved another letter. "Here's someone who wants to know Donny's favorite joke."

"That's the third question about jokes," Jessica said. "And there are six questions about his favorite movie star and two about his scariest experience. With so many repeats, we'll probably have room to answer everybody's questions."

"I like this one," Kimberly said, reading another letter. "'Dear Donny, I'm curious about your love life. Please describe your perfect date.'" She looked around at her friends. "How do you think Donny would answer that?"

Lila leaned back and closed her eyes as if she were meditating on the answer. "Dear Curious, My love life is a deep, dark secret," she said, opening her eyes. "I never tell anybody about it. But I can tell you that I would never pass up a date with a girl who is pretty, popular, wears the best clothes, and belongs to the best clubs. I like brown-haired girls best of all." Lila's hair was brown.

"No way, Lila," Jessica objected. "We're not going to put that in—the part about the brown hair, I mean. I'm *sure* Donny likes blonds better."

"Here's another," Ellen broke in. "'Dear Donny, I'm worried about my boyfriend. He's very jealous of the cute boy who sits next to me in homeroom. I can't even talk to this guy without my boyfriend getting mad. How would you handle this situation?'"

Jessica smiled. "Dear Terribly Worried," she said, "This isn't such a problem! If your boyfriend is jealous, it proves he really loves you. In fact, why don't you try to make him even *more* jealous? That way you'll know how much he cares." She looked at the letter more closely. "I wonder who wrote this," she added.

Kimberly shook her head. "That's a dumb answer, Jess," she declared. "Guys get jealous when they think you *don't* care about them. I think Donny ought to say something like this." She looked up at the ceiling, collecting her thoughts. "Dear Worried, Your boyfriend is jealous because you're not paying enough attention to him. If you let him know you really care about him, he'll stop worrying. That way, you can pay as much attention as you want to the cute guy in your homeroom."

Jessica giggled. "Maybe we should give Donny's column a new name—Donny Diamond Talks About Romance."

"Or, Donny Diamond Solves Your Love Problems," Kimberly suggested.

"Hey, everybody, listen to *this* letter," Mary said, suddenly serious. "'Dear Donny, Your interview was very interesting. But I don't believe the Unicorns really know you. I hope I'm wrong. Of course, all you have to do to prove it is to print a photograph of you and the Unicorns together.'"

Jessica snatched the letter out of Mary's hand. "It's typed," she told the others, "and there's no signature." She glared at the letter. "Who would write something like this?"

"Do you suppose somebody's figured out the truth?" Mary asked, sounding scared.

Lila took the letter away from Jessica with a knowing look. "I'll tell you exactly who wrote this," she said. "Elizabeth and the *Sixers*, that's who. They're the ones in this school who are really jealous."

"But what should we do about it?" Kimberly asked.

"I think we should just ignore it," Lila said with a shrug.

"Lila's right," Ellen agreed. "We should throw junk like this away. The *Sixers* are just worried that our Donny Diamond stuff is better than anything in their nerdy little paper, that's all."

Jessica took the letter back and read it again. She was beginning to feel very angry. If Elizabeth and the *Sixers* sent the letter, she knew the perfect way to get back at them.

She smiled. "I've got a better idea," she said. "Something that will surprise *everybody*—especially the person who wrote this letter."

"There are piles of our papers *everywhere*," Sophia said solemnly. It was lunchtime the following Wednesday. The third edition of the Unicorns' paper, featuring the 'Dear Donny' column, had come out the day before. When Elizabeth and Amy distributed the *Sixers* Wednesday morning, nobody seemed very interested in reading it. And at the beginning of lunch period, there were still stacks of papers at all of the distribution points.

"Nobody cares about the *Sixers* anymore," Nora said in a gloomy voice. "Everybody's still talking about the Unicorns' paper."

"I don't see what's so great about their stupid paper, anyway," Amy replied grouchily. "There's hardly any news in it. Just that stupid picture, that's all. I can't believe that everybody's so excited about a *picture*."

"And you can't even *see* the picture," Nora reminded her. "Not very well, anyway. The photocopy is awfully blurry."

"You can sure read the caption, though," Elizabeth said. Elizabeth could quote that caption word for word. It read, *You asked for it, so here it is, our latest club photo. Donny Diamond has just agreed to become an honorary Unicorn.* The picture showed all of the Unicorns, with Donny Diamond in the middle. It was blurred, but that didn't matter to most people. They were all amazed and envious of the Unicorns. Imagine having your picture taken with Donny Diamond!

"You know," Amy said thoughtfully, "this whole thing is pretty strange. I wonder how they got the answers to those questions so fast. And when did the Unicorns get their picture taken with Donny Diamond? It must have been sometime last week because they didn't say anything about Donny being an honorary Unicorn in last week's paper."

"Amy's right," Nora chimed in. "Did Donny come to Sweet Valley to get his picture taken with them? Or did they go to his house?"

"And if they *did* go to his house," Amy went on, "when did they do it?" She shook her head. "If you ask me, there's something very suspicious about this."

Elizabeth frowned. "I agree," she said. "But proving that the picture and the other stuff are fakes would be almost impossible."

"It would be difficult," Amy agreed. "But if we could do it, they'd have to stop printing that stuff. And then people would start reading the *Sixers* again."

"Especially since the *Sixers* is free," Nora added.

"Yeah," Amy said. "I wonder why the Unicorns decided to charge money for their paper. It must keep *some* people from reading it, and I doubt they're making much money."

"Let's figure it out," Elizabeth suggested. "They're charging fifteen cents for each copy, and they've probably sold three hundred copies." She penciled a quick calculation on her paper napkin. "That's *forty-five* dollars, minus whatever it cost for the photocopying."

"Forty-five dollars!" Nora said with a gasp. "Wow, that's a lot of money."

"It sure is," Elizabeth said grimly. She shook her head stubbornly. "I think we'd better try to do a better job with the *Sixers*. If we do, maybe people will start reading it again."

"A better job?" Sophia asked in a doubtful tone. "Are you sure we should even bother putting out a paper next week?"

Amy gave a short laugh. "We could just put the one from *this* week out again. Nobody would know the difference."

Nora and Sophia laughed weakly. But Elizabeth gave them a firm look.

"The track meet is coming up," she said, "and everybody likes to read about sports. Let's do a big feature on the track team."

Nora looked hopeful. "That ought to work. If anything will," she added.

"I guess," Sophia said in a resigned voice.

"I still think we ought to do some investigating," Amy said. "If we can figure out some way to prove that the Unicorns are printing lies, everyone will stop reading their paper."

"The only thing I want to figure out," Elizabeth responded, "is how to get our readers back."

"I can't believe it," Ellen said after Mary had given the treasurer's report at the Unicorn meeting that night. "We've actually made forty-five dollars? From just *one* week's edition of the newspaper?"

"That means in two weeks we could make nearly a hundred dollars," Kimberly said.

"We could use the money to buy tickets to the next Donny Diamond concert," Jessica suggested.

"Or we could throw a huge party," Ellen added.

"We could buy Unicorn Club jackets for everyone," Tamara put in.

"Don't forget to subtract the money we spent on printing the paper," Mary added.

Janet cleared her throat. "We can get back to that in a minute," she said. "Right now, let's talk about the dance."

Jessica smiled. If there was anything more exciting than the newspaper, it was the dance.

"The publicity committee," Janet announced, "has had posters printed advertising the dance and the mystery guest. People are already curious about the mystery guest, so tickets are selling fast. In fact, ticket sales are going so well that we'll be able to spend a little more on the band and the refreshments."

"Who *is* the mystery guest, Lila?" Kimberly asked.

"Yes," Janet said, "we'd all like to know. Who is it?"

Lila gave them a mysterious look. "You'll just have to wait and see," she said.

"You mean you won't tell us?" Ellen asked. She sounded hurt. "You don't trust us?"

Jessica laughed. "Are you kidding? Look at the way the news leaked out about our Donny Diamond interview. I agree with Lila. She shouldn't even tell *us* who it is. Even if we are dying to know," she added.

Lila gave Jessica a grateful glance.

"Oh, all right," Janet agreed. "I guess we'll just have to wait and find out. Now, I think we should thank Jessica for the wonderful way she's handling the newspaper. The photo was excellent, Jessica. And so was the caption. Donny Diamond, honorary Unicorn. I love it."

"I've looked at the picture dozens of times," Kimberly told Jessica, "and I still can't guess how you did it. It looks so *real*."

"Oh, it wasn't hard," Jessica said modestly. "Do you remember that picture we had taken last summer with Janet's brother Sam? Well, all I did was paste a small magazine photo of Donny's head onto Sam's body."

"Well, however you did it," Janet said, "it was

great." She sighed happily. "*Everybody's* talking about the Unicorns and Donny Diamond."

"I still think it's unbelievable," Ellen said, shaking her head. "Forty-five dollars from one little newspaper! Jessica, you're wonderful!"

Being editor-in-chief of the newspaper is definitely a terrific job, Jessica thought happily.

Eight

◇

"Let's walk home together," Lila whispered to Jessica after the Unicorn meeting. "I have to talk to you. Alone." That immediately got Jessica's attention.

"What's up?" Jessica demanded as soon as she and Lila were outside.

"Oh, nothing much," Lila replied casually. "Except I have a small problem, and I was hoping you could help me with it."

Now Jessica was really interested. Lila almost never told anybody about her problems. She liked her friends to know when things were going right, but hated it if they knew when something went wrong.

"What is it?" Jessica asked, trying not to sound too eager.

"Well, it's just that my uncle hasn't located a mystery guest yet," Lila confessed. "I'm sure he'll come up with somebody soon," she added quickly. "In fact, I'll probably get a phone call from him tonight. But I wondered if you had any ideas about who we could get. As a backup, I mean."

"No mystery guest?" Jessica exclaimed. "But you told Janet—"

Lila gave a light little laugh. "What Janet doesn't know won't hurt her. Anyway, we'll get it worked out right away, I'm sure." She paused. "So what do you think?" she asked in an offhand way. "Do you have any ideas?"

"Why hasn't your uncle found anybody yet?" Jessica asked. She was beginning to get this terrible feeling. "Didn't you ask him?"

Lila avoided Jessica's eyes. "Of course I asked him," she said uncomfortably. "But he—well, I've called him a couple of times but he just hasn't done anything about it yet. He's a very busy man with a lot of important clients to take care of, but he'll definitely come through," she added hastily. "I still think it would be a good idea if we had somebody else as a backup, just in case." She threw Jessica an almost pleading look. "Well, what do you think, Jessica? Can you suggest anybody?"

Jessica could hardly believe what Lila was telling her. Even though this wasn't the first time Lila's bragging had gotten her into trouble, it *was* the first time it had gotten the entire Unicorn Club into trouble. If Lila didn't come up with a good mystery guest, the kids who had bought dance tickets would riot. Janet would be furious. And it would all be Lila's fault. Lila *had* to come up with a mystery guest, and in spite of Lila's claim that her uncle would come through, it looked as if she might have to do it without his help.

Jessica shook her head slowly. "I wish I could suggest somebody, Lila, but I can't. I mean, there's just nobody in Sweet Valley who would be a good mystery guest."

Lila was losing her casual tone. "But you've *got* to help me!" she exclaimed. "We've got to come up with somebody."

"Why don't you ask your committee for suggestions?" Jessica asked.

Lila looked down at the ground. "Because my committee thinks my uncle already got someone," she said in a muffled voice.

Jessica sighed. Lila had obviously told her

committee the same thing she'd told Janet and the rest of the Unicorns. If she asked them for their help, she'd have to confess that she had lied. And Lila would never do that.

"Well, let me think about it," Jessica said slowly.

Lila brightened. "Oh, thank you, Jessica," she said, sounding relieved. "I just *knew* you'd come up with something! Listen, call me just as soon as you think of somebody. OK?"

"Hey, wait a minute, Lila," Jessica objected. "This is *your* problem, not mine. Remember? You're the chairman of the music committee."

"But you always have such fabulous ideas," Lila said smoothly. She was back to her old self again. "Your newspaper idea, for instance." She smiled a confident smile. "I'm sure you'll come up with a wonderful idea for a mystery guest, Jess."

But Jessica was not at all sure. There was a nervous feeling in the pit of her stomach. What if she and Lila could not come up with a mystery guest? What would they do then?

"Hi," Jessica said, walking into the P.E. office the following morning. "What did you want to see me about, Ms. Langberg?" Ms. Langberg was Jessica's gym teacher. At the beginning of gym that day, she had asked Jessica to come talk to her when class was over.

Jessica knew she hadn't done anything wrong—at least, nothing that Ms. Langberg knew about. But all through class, Jessica had watched Ms. Langberg's face and nervously tried to figure out what she wanted.

"Sit down, Jessica," Ms. Langberg said. She took out the last issue of The *Middle School News*. "I hear you're the editor of the Unicorns' newspaper."

Jessica sat down, suddenly feeling very nervous. "Yes, I am," she said. Why did Ms. Langberg want to talk about the newspaper?

"I think it's fascinating," Ms. Langberg said, "that you and the other Unicorns have been able to become friends with Donny Diamond. I've been a big fan of his for a long time, and I've followed his career with interest. How did you get to know him, Jessica?"

Jessica was surprised to find out that a *teacher* liked Donny Diamond.

"Lila Fowler's uncle is in the record business," Jessica said. "He introduced us and gave us Donny's home phone number. Then we called him and he agreed to let us interview him over the phone." This was the same story the Unicorns had agreed to tell any of their friends who asked.

"And the photograph?" Ms. Langberg pressed. "When was it taken?"

"Oh, a few days ago," Jessica said nervously. It was one thing to put the picture in the newspaper; it was another to lie about it to a teacher. "You see," she added uneasily, "he was so pleased with the way we did the interview that he suggested the 'Dear Donny' column."

"He did?" Ms. Langberg asked. She sounded impressed.

"Uh-huh," Jessica said. She wanted to get out of there immediately, but Ms. Langberg seemed to want to hear more about Donny Diamond. *She must really be a big fan of his,* Jessica thought. *Maybe she even has a crush on him!* Under other circumstances, that thought would have been terribly amusing to Jessica. But just then, it didn't even seem funny.

"Go on, Jessica," Ms. Langberg urged. "Tell me all about it. It's such an amazing story, it's almost unbelievable."

"Well, there's nothing to tell really," Jessica said. "We asked him questions and he answered them. And then he suggested that we all take a picture together as a reminder of the good time we had together." Jessica was expanding the story the Unicorns had agreed on to make it sound more believable. "Donny's really nice," she added. "He's already promised he'll keep writing his column for us as long as people have questions to ask him."

"Isn't that utterly incredible?" Ms. Langberg murmured. "I mean, a good-looking, famous young man like that, who's involved in so many other things—Why, I think it's wonderful that he's willing to help the Unicorns this way."

"Yes, it *is* wonderful," Jessica said. For a second, she had the feeling that Ms. Langberg was making fun of her. But how could that be true? Anyway, she was so nervous by that time she could barely stand it. She had to get out of there. "If you don't mind," she said, "I have to get to my next class."

"But the next period is lunch," Ms. Langberg reminded her. "And I want to hear more about Donny Diamond and the Unicorns." She smiled. "I think I might have a question to ask him. He could probably give me some very good advice."

"I'd love to stay and talk, but I promised the Unicorns I'd eat lunch with them," Jessica said, trying not to sound desperate. "Maybe you can send in your question."

"Yes, of course I can," Ms. Langberg said. She gave Jessica a long, steady look. "All right, Jessica, you can go now," she finally said. "Thanks for stopping in. And thank you for letting me know the details of your relationship with Donny Diamond. As a longtime fan of his, I find it all very interesting."

"Oh, that's all right," Jessica said, getting up quickly. "I'm glad to talk about Donny anytime."

When Jessica got out into the hallway, she breathed a huge sigh of relief. Then she began to get worried, remembering Ms. Langberg's strange behavior. She could swear the gym teacher knew something that she was holding back from Jessica. But what could it be?

Well, there was no point in being worried over nothing, Jessica told herself. Anyway, she had to find Lila and Ellen, and tell them the news. Their gym teacher had a *crush* on Donny Diamond!

The mail kept pouring in. There were dozens and dozens of 'Dear Donny' letters in response to the last issue of The *News*.

At first, the Unicorns were delighted. But

they slowly realized they had already answered all of the easy questions about Donny, and this new group of questions would be much more difficult.

"Listen to this one," Kimberly said. "'Dear Donny, I own all of your albums, but I'd love to hear you perform in person. When will you be having a concert in Sweet Valley?'"

"We can't answer that," Ellen said. "We don't know when he'll be here or if he'll be here."

"I know you guys will think I'm crazy, but I hope he never comes," Mary said slowly. "What if somebody asked him about the Unicorns and he said he never heard of us!"

"That's ridiculous, Mary," Jessica said, even though she didn't really think so. "Nobody would ask Donny Diamond a question like that!"

"Why not?" Mary persisted.

"Just because," Jessica said angrily. She reached for the letter. "Let's just say Donny will be here—soon. We don't have to give an exact date."

Another person wrote in to ask what kind of car Donny drove. Even Lila had to admit that she didn't know, and she couldn't find the answer in any of her rock magazines.

"Let's just say that Donny has six cars in his garage," Jessica decided at last, "but that he is so busy that he hardly has time to drive any of them."

"Six cars?" Kimberly asked. "Isn't that an awful lot?"

"Not for a rock star," Jessica replied. "Rock stars always have a lot of cars."

"These questions are really hard," Mary said. "I hope they start getting easier."

But they didn't. The worst letter of all arrived the day before the next issue of *The Middle School News* was due to come out.

"I was kind of expecting this," Mary said unhappily as she handed a letter to Jessica.

Jessica unfolded the letter. It was typed and unsigned just like the one demanding the photograph of Donny Diamond with the Unicorns. It said, *Dear Unicorns, I have to give you an A for effort. But the picture of Donny Diamond was a fake. You're just pretending to know him. Here's a question for you. You'd better answer it quick, before you get yourselves into big trouble. How far can you go before you get caught?*

Jessica angrily crumpled the paper into a little ball. She was convinced that her twin had sent both letters. *An A for effort*, Jessica thought in disgust, *that sounds just like my dear sister.*

Nine

◇

Jessica had just paid for her milk when Elizabeth came up behind her in the cafeteria. "I think we ought to have a talk," Elizabeth said. "I have something to tell you."

"Oh, really," Jessica said, raising her eyebrows. It had been a long time since the twins had said more to each other than "Pass the salt" or "Mom says the phone's for you." "What could *you* have to say to *me*?" Jessica asked her twin now.

"Something important," Elizabeth replied calmly.

Elizabeth really did have something important to tell her sister, but it had taken her the whole morning to decide to do it. After all, Jessica had gotten herself into this mess by trying to hurt Elizabeth. But after she thought about it, Elizabeth realized that she was not even mad at Jessica anymore. And once she realized that, she knew what she ought to do.

"Listen, Elizabeth, I know exactly what you're going to tell me," Jessica said, walking toward a table. She glanced at Elizabeth with an air of superiority. "I guessed a long time ago."

"You did?" Elizabeth asked in surprise. She sat down and started to unwrap her lunch. "Well, I'm glad that you already know. What are you going to do about it?"

Jessica looked puzzled for a second, but when she started to speak, she sounded very angry. "Well, first I'm going to tell you exactly what I think of you," she said in a rush. "I think that writing those letters was a dirty, low-down trick. You only did it because you were jealous. And if you think you can scare the Unicorns by—"

Elizabeth held up a hand, completely confused. "Wait a minute, Jessica. I don't think we're talking about the same thing. I didn't write any letters."

"Don't play dumb with me, Elizabeth Wakefield," Jessica snapped. "You do *too* know what I'm talking about! I'm talking about those letters that you wrote to the 'Dear Donny' column. If you think you're going to scare us—"

"I don't know anything about any letters," Elizabeth broke in, shaking her head. "I came over here to warn you about the rumors I've been hearing since your paper came out this morning. And to say that I think we ought to stop fighting."

"—you're badly mistaken!" Jessica declared. "The Unicorns don't scare easily." She stopped and looked at her sister. "Rumors?" she asked. "What rumors?"

Elizabeth knew that the word "rumor" would get her twin's attention. Jessica always worried about what people were talking about, especially if she thought they might be talking about her.

Elizabeth leaned forward and lowered her voice so that nobody else could hear her.

"It's about the dance. People have been seeing the posters—you know, the ones announcing the mystery guest. They've also been reading your 'Dear Donny' column, where Donny announced that he'll be in Sweet Valley *soon*."

"So?" Jessica asked. "We want people to see the posters. And the more people who read the 'Dear Donny' column, the better." She gave Elizabeth a smug smile. "Of course, I can see how you wouldn't agree, Lizzie. You're just jealous because—"

"Wait, there's more," Elizabeth told her, calmly ignoring her last comment. She was determined not to fight anymore. "Everybody also knows that the president of the Unicorns is in charge of the dance. They've been reading that the Unicorns are friends with Donny, and they believe it, especially since they saw that picture of Donny and the Unicorns that you printed last week."

Jessica's smug look faded and she busied herself with opening her milk. "Why don't you just get to the point, Elizabeth," she said, still not looking at her sister.

Elizabeth put her hand on Jessica's arm. "Everybody's expecting Donny Diamond to be the mystery guest at the school dance," she said quietly.

For a long time, Jessica stared at Elizabeth. Then she swallowed.

"But . . . but, that's just plain crazy," she exclaimed. She gave a weak laugh. "Donny Diamond, at a Sweet Valley Middle School dance? You've *got* to be kidding. Nobody would believe a thing like that!"

"It may sound ridiculous," Elizabeth said with a shrug, "but rumors usually are. Anyway, everyone seems to believe it." She leaned back in her chair. "What are you going to do?"

"Do?" Jessica asked. Her voice came out as a high squeak. "Why should I do anything? It's just a stupid rumor, isn't it?" She paused. "And don't try to change the subject, Elizabeth. We were talking about those letters." She was trying to sound furious, but Elizabeth could see that she was thinking about something else. The news about the rumor had obviously upset her.

"Jessica," Elizabeth said, "I think everyone will be pretty upset when they get to the dance and find out that Donny Diamond isn't going to be there. I mean, they're paying a lot of money for those tickets, and—"

Jessica jumped up from her seat. "Elizabeth Wakefield, you can't play innocent with me," she said. "I refuse to sit here and listen to any more of it." She picked up her tray.

"Jessica—" Elizabeth began. But she never got to finish. Jessica was already gone.

It took Jessica five full minutes to find Lila. While she was searching, Bruce Patman stopped her in the hallway. "Good work!" he said. Normally, Jessica would have been thrilled to talk to Bruce, but just then she had a sinking feeling that she didn't want to know what he meant by "good work." "I've got to go," she mumbled, and practically ran down the hall away from him. By the time Jessica found Lila, she was feeling almost sick.

"Lila," Jessica exclaimed breathlessly, "I've been looking everywhere for you! I've got something really important to tell you."

"Did you get Elizabeth to confess to writing the letters?" Lila asked. "Mary told me that you were talking to her a few minutes ago."

"Elizabeth says she doesn't know anything about the letters," Jessica said in a rush. "But that's not what I want to tell you."

"I don't believe her," Lila said. "Nobody but Elizabeth has any reason to—"

"That's not important right now," Jessica broke in. "We've got a bigger problem. Have you heard the rumor about the dance?"

"What rumor?" Lila asked.

"The rumor that Donny Diamond is the mystery guest!" Quickly, Jessica repeated what Elizabeth had told her. As Jessica talked, Lila's eyes got bigger and bigger and her mouth dropped open.

"But people can't believe a thing like that!" she exclaimed when Jessica was finished. "It's ridiculous."

"It may be ridiculous," Jessica said miserably, "but they believe it anyway."

Lila looked horrified. "But we don't even *have* a mystery guest yet!" she wailed. "Unless my uncle comes through at the last minute. Or unless you've thought of somebody we can ask."

"I haven't thought of anybody," Jessica said. "But you and I are the only ones who know we don't have a guest. Everybody else thinks it's going to be Donny Diamond!"

Lila's face was white. "We've got to come up with someone fast, Jessica," she whispered.

"Lila," Jessica said, a look of horror on her face, "do you think everyone is expecting to hear Donny Diamond? What if they demand their money back when he doesn't show up?"

"I hate to say it," Lila said, "but I think we'd better go talk to Janet. She might be able to think of something."

When Lila and Jessica found Janet and told her what they had heard, she didn't sound at all worried about the rumors.

"As a matter of fact," she said, adding a few bills to the neat pile in front of her, "a few rumors are good for business. Ticket sales are excellent, especially today's. This is going to be the biggest dance ever!"

"But you don't understand," Jessica said, feeling panicked. Why wouldn't Janet listen? "People are buying all those tickets because they think Donny Diamond is the mystery guest!"

"And he *isn't*, of course," Lila said, sounding unhappy. "As a matter of fact, the mystery guest . . . I mean . . ." Her voice trailed off and she looked at Jessica helplessly.

Jessica swallowed hard. "What Lila's trying to say is that her uncle—"

"I'm sure," Janet said, "that Lila's uncle has come up with somebody really spectacular. When the kids see who your mystery guest is, Lila, they'll forget all about this Donny Diamond nonsense."

Lila tried again. "But the mystery guest—"

Janet raised her hand. "I don't want to know who it is," she said firmly. "If you tell me and it leaks out somehow, you'll think I'm the one who told. So I don't want to know."

"Do you think," Jessica asked timidly, "that people will be upset and demand that we give them their money back?"

Janet frowned. "I just don't understand what

you're so worried about," she replied. "*I* never said that Donny Diamond was going to appear at the dance. *None* of the Unicorns have ever said so. You didn't say it in the newspaper, either. Nobody can accuse us of trying to fool them. So what's the problem?"

"But people are expecting—" Jessica began.

"So what?" Janet replied impatiently. "It's not *our* fault that people have gotten it into their heads that Donny Diamond's going to be here." She gave an amused chuckle and went back to counting the ticket money. "Really, people are *so* gullible. They'll believe anything, no matter how ridiculous it is. Imagine, people thinking that Donny Diamond is going to play for a middle school dance."

"Well, Janet was a huge help," Lila said bitterly as she and Jessica walked toward their next class. "What do you think we should do now?"

"Well, I know exactly what *I'm* going to do," Jessica replied. "I'm going to clobber Elizabeth."

"Elizabeth?" Lila said. "What does Elizabeth have to do with this?"

"What do you mean, what does she have to do with it? This whole mess is Elizabeth's fault!" Jessica replied hotly. "If she hadn't left the Unicorns out of the *Sixers*, we'd never have started our own newspaper. And then none of this would ever have happened!"

"I really wish none of it ever had," Lila sighed.

Ten

◇

Jessica and Elizabeth were setting the table for dinner that night when Steven came home.

"Hey, Jessica," he said, "I have to tell you about this fantastic rumor that's going around Sweet Valley High. I thought it sounded ridiculous, but everybody else seems to be taking it seriously."

"People who believe rumors are dumb," Jessica said as calmly as she could. But there was an ache in the pit of her stomach. She had a terrible feeling that she knew what Steven was about to say.

"But lots of people believe this rumor, Jessica. *Smart* people," Steven said seriously. "You see, Anita Pearce's little sister, Caroline, told her that

Donny Diamond is a good friend of the Unicorns."

Elizabeth glanced at her sister. "Caroline Pearce is the biggest gossip in Sweet Valley," Elizabeth said coolly. "She doesn't always get her facts straight."

"Anita didn't believe her either, at first," Steven continued. "She thought it was dumb. But then Caroline showed her the picture of Donny and the Unicorns that you ran in your paper, and it convinced her. So when Anita found out from her sister that Donny's going to be the mystery guest at the next middle school dance, she told some of her friends. And now the rumor's all over Sweet Valley High."

The tips of Jessica's fingers felt numb. "Well, can't people see what a crazy rumor it is?" Jessica asked.

"Why would they think it's crazy?" Steven asked in his most innocent voice. "I mean, if Donny's as big a pal of the Unicorns as they say he is, the idea's very logical. In fact, it's so logical that some of the high school kids are getting their little brothers and sisters to buy them tickets to the middle school dance, just so they can see Donny. Jessica, your dance is going to be a sellout!"

Jessica groaned. "Well, they're wasting their

money. No one ever said that Donny Diamond would be there."

But that did not stop Steven. He was obviously going to torment Jessica as long as he could. "You see, Jessica, people have been reading the 'Dear Donny' column in your newspaper," he said. "Even kids at Sweet Valley High." He shook his head. "To think that my baby·sister can get Donny Diamond to write a column for her newspaper! It's absolutely incredible! Some of the answers are really kind of surprising, though. Like the one about Donny having six cars in his garage. He must have bought them in the last couple of weeks. This month's *Sports Car* magazine quotes him as saying, 'I love my antique Chevy convertible and I'd never own anything else.'"

Jessica dropped her handful of silverware. "Would you mind finishing for me, Liz?" she asked hurriedly. "I just realized I have a really urgent phone call to make."

"Wait, Jess," Steven called as Jessica rushed from the room. "I want to know more about Donny! I want you to ask him a question for me!"

"Oh, shut up, Steven," Elizabeth said.

Jessica dashed to the telephone to call Lila. When Lila answered, Jessica gasped, "Oh, Lila, the most awful thing has happened!"

"You're telling me?" Lila asked, in a doom-stricken voice. "My uncle just called."

Jessica could tell by the tone of Lila's voice that the call had not been good news. "What did he say?" she asked.

"He said," Lila replied, "that he'd forgotten all about our mystery guest until today. He apologized and explained that it's too late to try to get anybody now. Jessica, we're not going to *have* a mystery guest! Not Donny Diamond, not *anybody*!"

"Oh, no!" Jessica moaned. "Lila, this is terrible!"

There was a silence. Then Lila said dully, "Well, aren't you going to tell me why you called?"

Jessica swallowed. "Steven says that the rumor about Donny being the mystery guest is all over Sweet Valley High. Some of the high school kids are even getting their middle school brothers and sisters to buy them tickets to the dance, just so they can hear him!"

There was another silence, a longer one. Finally Jessica asked, "Lila? Are you there? Lila?"

"I'm here," Lila said with a sigh. "But I wish I weren't."

*   *   *

Jessica would never have guessed it was possible, but the next day, things got worse. Lila and Jessica were just leaving gym class when Ms. Langberg motioned to them to come into the office.

"I wish I didn't have to ask you this," she said when Jessica and Lila were sitting in front of her, "but I've been hearing some very upsetting rumors. A friend of mine who teaches at Sweet Valley High tells me that she's hearing them, too." She glanced from one to the other. "Do you know what I'm talking about, girls?"

Jessica and Lila exchanged looks of innocence. "Rumors?" Lila asked sweetly. "I don't remember hearing any rumors. How about you, Jessica?"

Jessica frowned, as if she were thinking very hard. "No," she said. "I don't. Of course," she added, "there's always so much gossip that nobody can remember all of it."

"Perhaps your memory needs a little help," Ms. Langberg said gently. "I'm speaking specifically of the rumors about the dance." When the girls still looked puzzled, she added, "About Donny Diamond."

Lila's expression cleared. "Oh, *those* rumors!" she exclaimed. She waved her hand. "They're so silly I'd forgotten all about them." She turned to Jessica. "You know, Jess. The rumors about Donny Diamond being the mystery guest."

Jessica tried to laugh, but it came out sounding strangled. "That dumb gossip? Oh, yes, I've heard that one. But it's so dumb that I forgot about it immediately."

"So people are mistaken," Ms. Langberg said. "Donny Diamond *isn't* going to be the mystery guest at the dance."

Both girls shook their heads without saying a word.

"How do you suppose that silly rumor got started?" Ms. Langberg asked.

"I have no idea," Lila said. "Some people are just very imaginative, I guess. Or maybe some people like to spread stories they know aren't true. Anyway, the Unicorns aren't responsible for what people are saying."

Jessica glanced at Lila in admiration. She was going to be tough. She wasn't going to admit anything.

Ms. Langberg turned to Jessica. "You don't think," she asked, "that it might have been that 'Dear Donny' column and the picture of Donny with the Unicorns that gave people the idea?"

Jessica tried to shrug, but it didn't quite come

off. "We never *said* that Donny Diamond was going to be the mystery guest," she replied uneasily.

Ms. Langberg pressed her lips together. "No, perhaps you never *said* that," she agreed. She leaned forward. "I want a straight answer. Now. Do you know Donny Diamond?"

Lila and Jessica glanced at each other. "Well," Lila began, "we certainly know all there is to know about—"

"That isn't what I mean," Ms. Langberg broke in sternly, "and you know it." She looked at Jessica. "Let me put it this way, Jessica. Have you ever personally met Donny Diamond? Did you actually have your picture taken with him?"

Feeling miserable, Jessica shook her head. What was Ms. Langberg going to do? Give them detentions? Ask the principal to *suspend* them?

"How about you, Lila?" Ms. Langberg asked. "Do you know Donny Diamond?"

After a minute, Lila shook her head too. "You see," she said in a choked voice, "the whole thing started out as a joke on Elizabeth and the *Sixers*. But it got out of hand, and we're terribly sorry. We know we were wrong." Her eyes were beginning to fill with tears.

"Lila's right," Jessica said sadly. "It was an

awful mistake from the very beginning, and we've been trying our best to get out of it." When she looked up, her eyes were filled with tears, too. "When the rumor started going around, we didn't know what to do. We knew we'd made a big mess, but we were in so deep that it was too late to change things. The last few days have been just miserable," she added, wiping the tears from her eyes. "We've been trying to figure out some way to tell people the truth."

"We've really learned our lesson," Lila added in her most virtuous voice. "We'll never do anything like this again. We can promise you that."

"Well, I can certainly sympathize," Ms. Langberg said. "Sometimes things don't turn out exactly the way we planned. And it's good that you can admit how wrong you were and feel bad about what you've done."

Lila and Jessica glanced at each other sideways. It looked as if they were going to get out of this thing after all!

Ms. Langberg clasped her hands on her desk. "Actually, the fact that you already see your mistake will make it easier for you to apologize."

"Apologize?" Jessica asked uneasily.

"Why, yes," Ms. Langberg said. "I'm sure

you want to let everyone at Sweet Valley Middle School know just how terrible you feel about everything that's happened."

"We do?" Lila asked, caught off guard. She collected herself. "I mean, of *course* we do."

Ms. Langberg beamed. "I'm delighted to know that you want to do the right thing. And I'm sure that you'll want to do it when everyone is together."

Jessica threw Lila a desperate look. What was Ms. Langberg getting at?

"That means, of course," Ms. Langberg continued, "that you'll want to take care of this little matter at the dance."

"At . . . at the dance?" Lila gasped.

"At the dance," Ms. Langberg replied. "That will be the perfect opportunity for you two girls to tell everyone that the Unicorns have never met Donny Diamond, and that all those 'Dear Donny' answers were fakes."

Jessica's heart nearly stopped beating. She was going to have to stand up in front of everybody at the dance and admit that she had never known Donny Diamond? That she had made up everything that went into the newspaper? She would rather do detention for ten weeks. She would rather be suspended. She would rather *die*!

"I'm sure that people will be angry and disappointed," Ms. Langberg said, "but they'll probably be willing to forgive you when you tell them how sorry you are for the trouble you've caused." Ms. Langberg smiled. "By the way, I understand that you're responsible for getting the mystery guest, Lila. Who is it?"

Lila chewed on her lip. After a few seconds she said, "Actually, we don't have one. My uncle was supposed to help me find somebody, but he couldn't. And now it's too late. Everybody's booked for that night."

"I see," Ms. Langberg replied. "Well, in that case, maybe I can help. I have a cousin in Santa Monica who does some singing. You know— weddings, bar mitzvahs, retirement parties, that sort of thing." She smiled. "He plays the accordian. I'm sure he'd be available for that night. He doesn't have many bookings, you see, and he's always glad to play. It gives him practice."

Jessica closed her eyes. An accordian player who needed practice? He sounded like an absolute dud. The nerdiest of the nerds. She tried frantically to think of an excuse to say no, but she was afraid to offend Ms. Langberg.

"Perhaps his kind of music is a little old-fashioned," Ms. Langberg admitted cheerfully.

"But it would be a shame not to give the kids something for their money. Anyway, it sounds like it's your only alternative, if everybody else is booked. What have you got to lose?"

"What have we got to lose?" Jessica echoed weakly. Mystery guest or no mystery guest, they were in for it. They were backed into a corner. They had to admit to inventing 'Dear Donny' and all the other stuff. *And* they had to listen to Ms. Langberg's nerdy cousin play his accordian. How horrible.

"Well, then, it's all settled," Ms. Langberg said, standing up. "What time would you like my cousin to come?"

"Just tell him to show up at nine o'clock," Lila said in an unenthusiastic voice. "And it doesn't really matter if he can't make it."

"Oh, I'm sure he'll be delighted to come," Ms. Langberg said, putting her hand on Lila's shoulder. "He might even be able to bring his friends."

"His . . . friends?" Jessica asked apprehensively.

"Yes," Ms. Langberg said. "He's been getting a group together, from what I understand." She smiled. "They call themselves Donald Kaminsky and the Polka Dots."

Eleven

◇

"What's wrong, Jess?" Elizabeth asked. "Are you sick?" The twins had to leave for the dance in less than an hour, and Jessica hadn't even started getting ready yet. Something was clearly wrong.

"I'm not sick," Jessica declared dramatically. "I'm dying." Her voice was muffled. She was lying on her bed with her head under a pillow.

Elizabeth was confused. Even though the twins had been getting along better that week, Jessica hadn't told Elizabeth anything about what was going to happen at the dance.

"Maybe it would help if you talked about it," Elizabeth said sympathetically. "It can't be that bad."

Jessica pulled the pillow off her head. "It's

worse than you think," she wailed, sitting up. "I have to *confess!*"

"Confess? Confess what?" Elizabeth asked.

"Ms. Langberg found out that we made all that stuff up, the interviews and the 'Dear Donny' letters," Jessica said sadly. "She's making Lila and me confess tonight at the dance, in front of everybody!" She flung herself back on the bed. "I'd rather *die!*" she groaned. Then she sat up again. "I hope I break a leg going down the stairs," she said. "Or maybe we'll have an accident on the way to the dance."

Elizabeth smothered a smile. It was just like Jess to try to imagine a dramatic way out of trouble. "You don't really want to break your leg," she said.

"Oh, yes, I do," Jessica said emphatically. She looked down at her legs. "I wonder if a broken leg hurts very much," she said. "I wonder if I'd limp a lot."

Elizabeth sat down on the bed. "Look, Jessica," she said encouragingly, "you've got to tell the truth sooner or later. You might as well get it over with."

"But I'll be so *humiliated!*" Jessica cried. She cast a look at herself in the mirror. "And I look *awful!*"

Without a word, Elizabeth went to her room, opened the closet, and took out her favorite blue cotton dress. It was one Jessica was always wanting to borrow because she thought it made her look more grown up. Elizabeth carried it back to Jessica's room.

"Here, Jess," she said. "You can wear my blue dress tonight."

Jess looked up. "I can?" she asked.

"And we'll put your hair up, too," Elizabeth told her, picking up the brush. "How would you like it? In a French braid?" That was the way Jessica liked to wear it for very special occasions.

Jessica moaned. "I guess," she said despondently. "But it won't make any difference how I look. When people hear my confession, they'll want to kill me!"

But after Jessica had seen the way she looked in Elizabeth's blue dress, she felt a little better. And after her twin had fixed her hair and had dabbed on some pale lip gloss, she began to feel quite a bit more cheerful.

A few minutes before she and Elizabeth were ready to go, Jessica called Lila.

"I'm sick," Lila announced. "I can't go to the dance tonight."

"Lila Fowler, you are *not* sick!" Jessica exclaimed indignantly. "You're just trying to avoid going."

"I am *too* sick," Lila insisted. "I get sick every time I think of having to listen to Donald Kaminsky and the Polka Dots."

"That kind of sick doesn't count," Jessica said firmly. "You have to get up there with me and take your share of the blame. Anyway," she added, "we've got to tell the truth sooner or later. We might as well get it over with."

There was a long silence. "I guess you're right," Lila finally agreed.

"We'll be there in ten minutes to pick you up. You'd better be ready," Jessica said sternly.

"But I *can't* be ready that soon!" Lila wailed. "My hair's a mess."

"Ten minutes," Jessica repeated.

Ten minutes later, Mrs. Wakefield pulled up in front of the Fowler mansion. Twenty minutes later, after Jessica had practically dragged Lila out of the house, they had arrived at the gym.

Jessica couldn't believe it when she saw how many people were there. The gym was packed wall-to-wall with kids. Most of them were from the middle school, but Jessica saw a few high school kids she recognized. The local band had already started to play, but not many people were dancing. Most of them were standing around in little groups, talking and looking at their watches. They were obviously waiting for Donny Diamond to arrive.

"Oh, Jessica, aren't you *excited*!" Caroline Pearce said, running up to Jessica and Lila. She closed her eyes. There was a blissful expression on her face and she was clasping Donny's latest album, *Roarin' Rock*. "I just can't believe that I'll be listening to Donny Diamond in just a few minutes." Her eyes flew open. "Do you think," she asked, "that I might actually *faint* when he starts to play?"

"Believe me, Caroline," Jessica said with a sigh, "you won't faint." It was not likely that Donald Kaminsky and the Polka Dots would affect Caroline Pearce so dramatically.

"I'm feeling really awful, Jessica," Lila said in a low voice, after Caroline had gone. "I can't take any more of this. I'm going to the rest room."

"I'm going with you," Jessica said, determined not to let Lila out of her sight. Not that she didn't trust her friend. It was just that . . . well, Lila might decide that she really *was* sick, call a taxi, and go home.

But things were not any better in the rest room. The two girls were immediately mobbed by crowds of Donny Diamond fans, spilling over with questions.

"Is he here yet?"

"Can you get him to sign my Donny Diamond T-shirt?"

"I brought my camera. Do you think you could get Donny to pose for a picture with me?"

Finally, Jessica and Lila pushed their way out of the rest room. "Isn't there *any* place we can get away from this?" Lila asked desperately. "It's humiliating to have so many people congratulating us."

"I don't know—" Jessica started to say.

But just then, the band stopped playing.

"It sounds like intermission," Jessica said in a whisper, "which means that it's time for the mystery guest. Come on, Lila. We've got to go tell people what happened."

"I can't," Lila whispered. "I'm scared!" Her eyes were wide with fear. "Jessica, what do you think they'll *do*?"

"I don't know," Jessica said. "I'm scared, too. But we have to do it anyway." She could hear the kids in the gym chanting, *We want Donny!*

When Jessica and Lila got backstage, they found Donald Kaminsky and the Polka Dots setting up. Somebody—probably Donald—was playing warm-up scales on an accordian. It was worse, much worse, than Jessica had imagined. The accordian player had strange, wooly red hair, and he was wearing a green plaid coat and a pair of nerdy green-rimmed glasses. And he had on a bow tie. A *polka-dot* bow tie!

"Oh, *no*," Lila moaned, shutting her eyes. She clutched at Jessica's hand. "Jessica, I think I'm going to faint."

"You can't faint now, Lila," Jessica said desperately. "We've got to go on stage first."

"Hello, girls," Ms. Langberg said, coming toward them with a bright smile on her face. "Donald says he and his band are ready whenever you are."

Jessica took a deep breath. "I guess we'd better get it over with," she said apprehensively.

When the kids saw Jessica and Lila stepping out in front of the microphone, they applauded wildly. When Jessica started talking, the applause quieted down. At first, when they heard what she was saying, they laughed. They seemed to think it was some sort of joke.

"This isn't a joke," Jessica said miserably. "It's true. The interview and the answers from Donny, we just made them up. We really don't know Donny at all."

"If you don't know him," somebody shouted from the audience, "how'd you get him to come to the dance tonight?"

"We didn't," Lila said. "Donny Diamond isn't going to be here. That was all just a rumor."

The audience remained quiet. They seemed to be whispering among themselves.

"A rumor?" somebody suddenly shouted. "You mean, I came here for nothing?" The gym began to echo with a chorus of loud, angry shouts and stamping feet.

"We want Donny!" everybody was yelling.

"What now?" Lila asked, looking as if she wanted to sink through the floor.

Jessica pulled the microphone away from Lila. "We *do* have a mystery guest, though," she said, hoping to quiet them down a little.

But it didn't work. "We want Donny!" the crowd kept on chanting. "We want Donny!"

"I'd like to introduce," Jessica shouted above the noise. "All the way from Santa Monica, Donald Kaminsky and the Polka Dots!"

"The Polka Dots?" somebody shouted incredulously. "Whoever heard of the Polka Dots? What is this, some kind of stupid joke?"

"We've been cheated!" somebody else yelled. "Give us our money back!"

Lila looked terrified. "I'm getting out of here," she said, and fled from the stage. Jessica hesitated for an instant, and then followed her.

At that moment, the curtains swept open and the crowd quieted down. Then, as people began to take in the sight of a red-haired character with an accordian, there were hoots of laughter. The laughter quickly turned to hissing.

"We want Donny! We want Donny!" the chanting began again.

The red-haired accordian player looked bewildered. "You want *who*?" he asked uncertainly, walking to the front of the stage and looking around. He put one hand behind his ear and bent forward, as if he couldn't hear what they were saying. "Who do you want?"

"We want Donny!" everybody shrieked madly. "DONNY DIAMOND!"

The accordian player grinned. "Why didn't you say so?" he asked. "If you want Donny Diamond, that's who you're going to get!"

And Donald Kaminsky ripped off his red wig and his polka-dot tie and grabbed an electric guitar that one of the band members tossed him. Then he ripped into the wildest version ever of "Hot Rockin' Tonight."

It was Donny Diamond!

Twelve

◇

"I'm going to faint," Jessica said happily, collapsing limply onto the bleachers.

"If you faint," Lila warned her, "you'll miss something!"

On stage, Donny was starting another song, and the kids were screaming wildly. A number of people had already come up to Jessica and Lila, thanking them for a great time. Even Janet had congratulated them on arranging a fantastic evening.

"I don't know how you two did it," Janet said. "But this whole evening is incredible. It's beyond my wildest dreams!"

"Beyond mine, too," Jessica admitted happily.

The evening that had started out like a nightmare was now a complete success.

Lila smiled calmly, as if she had known all along that things were going to turn out just fine.

Jessica was amazed at what had happened. To her surprise, everybody seemed convinced that their confession about the newspaper had been some kind of crazy stunt, like Donny's ridiculous costume. Nobody seemed to believe a word of what she had said. After all, the Unicorns had brought Donny to Sweet Valley, hadn't they? How could they have convinced him to come if they had never met him before tonight? Everybody was asking when the next edition of The *Middle School News* was coming out, so they could read all about the dance. And lots of kids were coming up with questions for the next 'Dear Donny' column!

Out on the gym floor, Elizabeth and Amy were listening to Donny, while all around them people buzzed about Jessica's terrific introduction. Of course, Caroline Pearce was helping spread the gossip. She had heard, she told everyone who would listen, that Jessica and Lila had been planning this for weeks and had suggested to Donny that he disguise himself in order to keep people guessing for a few minutes longer.

"You know," Amy said, shaking her head, "you've got to hand it to Jessica. She always manages to come out on top. How in the world did she and Lila get Donny Diamond here, especially if they'd never met him?"

Elizabeth grinned. She'd been proud that Jessica had had the courage to stand up in front of everybody and admit what she and the other Unicorns had done. She knew how embarrassed Jessica must have felt. She *did not* know how Donny Diamond had shown up. And from the look of surprise on her twin's face when Donny Diamond started to play, she didn't think Jessica had expected him either.

But Elizabeth was glad things had turned out this way. Let people think whatever they wanted to about the way things happened tonight. Jessica had suffered enough. Maybe she had even learned a lesson, for once!

"Jessica, Lila," Ms. Langberg motioned to them from backstage. "Come here. There's someone I'd like you to meet."

Jessica could hardly believe her eyes. Donny Diamond was even cuter in real life than he was in his pictures.

"Jessica Wakefield and Lila Fowler, I'd like

you to meet my cousin Donald Kaminsky. Donald, this is Jessica and Lila, the girls I told you about," Ms. Langberg said.

"Donald *Kaminsky*?" Lila shrieked.

Donny grinned. "Donny Diamond sounds a lot better, doesn't it?" His grin faded. "My cousin sent me copies of your newspaper because she thought I ought to see them. When I read what you'd written about me, I decided to send you a letter, and sort of put you on the spot."

"So *you're* the one who wrote those two letters!" Jessica whispered.

"After all, you were using my name, *without* my permission," Donny replied sternly. "I was flattered that you liked me so much that you'd bother to invent stories about me. But I didn't think you were being honest or fair with your readers, especially when I learned that your club was making money out of the lies you were telling about me."

Jessica felt her face get hot. It was terrible to hear Donny describe what they had written as "lies." But she had to admit that it was true.

"Anyway," Donny said, "when I heard about the mystery-guest rumor that was going around, I decided to help out." He gave Jessica and Lila a hard look. "I thought it was important for you girls to learn a lesson first, but not at the expense of other people."

Jessica nodded. She had learned a lesson—the *hard* way. Standing up in front of that crowd to confess was the toughest thing she'd ever done in her entire life. She would never forget how mortified she had felt.

"I've been thinking," she said soberly, "that it's not right for the Unicorns to keep the money we got from the newspaper."

Donny smiled approvingly. "That's a good thought, Jessica. What could you do with it?"

"We could put it in the class trip fund," she said.

"Or maybe we could give it to the principal to buy some new equipment," Lila put in.

Donny nodded. "Those are both good ideas. And what about your newspaper?"

Jessica bit her lip. "There's not going to be a newspaper anymore," she said.

"Good again," Donny said. He picked up his guitar. "Well, before I go, there's one thing I would like, if you don't mind."

"What's that?" Jessica and Lila chorused eagerly.

"I'd like you to round up the Unicorns so we can all have our picture taken together." He grinned and put his arm around Jessica's shoulder. "After all, that last photo was terribly blurry. If I'm going to be an honorary Unicorn, I want to have a good picture of the club!"

Now Jessica really *did* think she was going to faint.

"I'm really sorry for everything, Lizzie," Jessica told her sister later that night. "I should have listened when you tried to tell me why you left my Unicorn story out of the *Sixers*."

"It was partly my fault, too," Elizabeth said. "I should have called you at Lila's the night before to tell you that the story wouldn't be there. And I shouldn't have lost my temper with you."

Jessica hugged her sister. "It's *horrible* to fight," she confessed. "Let's not do it again, OK?"

"Well, let's *try* not to do it again," Elizabeth said with a giggle.

"I've got a little present for you," Jessica said. She held up the latest Donny Diamond album. "Donny gave me a copy of his newest album, and I asked him to autograph it for you."

"Oh, Jessica," Elizabeth said happily. "Thank you!"

Jessica heaved a dramatic sigh. "So I guess

this is the end of my career in newspapers," she said.

"It doesn't have to be," Elizabeth told her with a smile. "Would you like to write a story about the Unicorns for the next edition of the *Sixers*?" she offered.

"No way!" Jessica said firmly, shaking her head. "The Unicorns have had enough publicity for a while."

Elizabeth's smile got bigger. "Well, then, how about a story about Donny Diamond's appearance at the dance?"

Jessica looked at her. "Hey!" she said excitedly, "that's an absolutely fantastic idea! Why didn't I think of it?" She reached for the phone. "Just wait until Lila hears this!"

Elizabeth shook her head, laughing. Jessica might have learned a lesson, but she was still the same Jessica!

After school the following Monday, Elizabeth and Amy were walking out of the door when they saw a cluster of kids standing beside the bike racks.

"I wonder what's going on," Elizabeth said to Amy.

"Let's go see."

The two girls walked over to the group. In the middle were Bruce Patman and Lois Waller. Bruce was sitting on his brand-new Italian racing bike, and Lois was holding her bike, which was older and beat up.

"How about a race, Lois?" Bruce said, with a nasty grin. A group of boys behind him laughed loudly.

Lois bit her lip. She looked very nervous. But she threw Bruce a challenging look. "I'm not going to race you, Bruce," she said. "Why should I? With that new bike of yours, you'd definitely win. All you want to do is show off."

That's it, Lois, Elizabeth thought. *Stand up for yourself!*

Bruce put on his most innocent look. "You've got it all wrong, Lois," he said. "I'm just doing this for your own good. If you raced, you might lose a pound or two." He looked at Charlie Cashman and Jerry McAllister. "How about it, guys? Don't you think Miss Roly Poly would look a lot better if she got rid of some of that excess fat?"

Jerry and Charlie snickered. "Well, let's just say it couldn't hurt," Jerry said.

"Jerry McAllister ought to watch what he's

saying about fat," Amy muttered. "He could stand to lose a few pounds himself."

Lois got on her bike, trying to ignore Bruce and his friends. But Bruce kept it up.

"Come on, dough girl," he urged her. "Just race me to the corner. Who knows, you might even win." He grinned. "I'll give you a head start," he added.

Lois looked uncertain. "Just to the corner?" she asked. "And after that I can go home?"

Elizabeth frowned. She knew what Lois was thinking. If she let Bruce have his way and raced him to the corner, he would be sure to win. Then he would be satisfied and leave her alone. But Elizabeth knew that Bruce would just come up with another way to torment her.

"Sure," Bruce said generously. "Sure. After that, you can go home and have a candy bar. Have *two* candy bars!" The boys hooted with laughter.

Her face bright red, Lois nodded slowly. "Well, I guess," she said. "As long as I get a head start."

"I wish she'd stand up to him," Amy told Elizabeth. "But the trouble is, it wouldn't do any good."

Elizabeth nodded silently.

"OK," Bruce called loudly, "it's race time! Somebody want to draw a starting line?"

Charlie Cashman took a piece of chalk out of his pocket and drew a line on the sidewalk. Jerry McAllister stood on one end and raised his hand. "Line up," he called.

Bruce and Lois wheeled their bikes to the line. Lois looked afraid. Bruce looked confident.

"I'll give two go's," Jerry said. "Lois, you go on the first one." He raised his hand.

Bruce braced one foot against the ground and the other on a pedal. He bent forward, tensing his muscles. Lois glanced at him. Then she did the same thing.

"Get set," Jerry called. He paused. "GO, Lois!"

Lois shoved her foot down and the pedal came off her bike. She shoved her other foot down and the other pedal came off. Then her bike tipped over and she landed flat on the ground.

Bruce, Charlie, and Jerry doubled over with uncontrolled laughter.

"Poor Lois," Bruce gasped pityingly, when he could catch his breath. "She broke her bike. It just wasn't strong enough to carry her weight."

Elizabeth bent over and helped Lois get up. "Don't pay any attention to him," she said angrily.

Lois was crying. "Oh, Elizabeth," she wailed. "Did I . . . did I really break my bike?"

Amy came over carrying the pedals that had come off. "It looks like somebody unbolted them," she said. "But there's no serious damage. I'll put them back on for you."

Elizabeth looked at Lois's tear-stained face. Maybe the bike wasn't damaged. But Lois was very upset.

Somebody has to do something about Bruce Pat-man, Elizabeth told herself. *But what?*

What will Lois do to get back at Bruce? Find out in Sweet Valley Twins #38, LOIS STRIKES BACK.

SWEET VALLEY TWINS™

Join Jessica and Elizabeth for
big adventure in exciting
SWEET VALLEY TWINS SUPER EDITIONS
and SWEET VALLEY TWINS CHILLERS.

☐ #1: CLASS TRIP   15588-1/$2.95
☐ #2: HOLIDAY MISCHIEF   15641-1/$2.95
☐ #3: THE BIG CAMP SECRET   15707-8/$2.95
☐ SWEET VALLEY TWINS SUPER SUMMER
FUN BOOK by Laurie Pascal Wenk
                                    15816-3/$3.50/3.95

Elizabeth shares her favorite summer projects &
Jessica gives you pointers on parties. Plus:
fashion tips, space to record your favorite
summer activities, quizzes, puzzles, a summer
calendar, photo album, scrapbook, address book
& more!

CHILLERS

☐ #1: THE CHRISTMAS GHOST 15767-1/$2.95
☐ #2: THE GHOST IN THE GRAVEYARD
                                    15801-5/$2.95

☐ #3: THE CARNIVAL GHOST   15859-7/$2.95

Bantam Books, Dept. SVT6, 414 East Golf Road, Des Plaines, IL 60016

Please send me the items I have checked above. I am enclosing $_____
(please add $2.00 to cover postage and handling). Send check or money
order, no cash or C.O.D.s please.

Mr/Ms _____

Address _____

City/State _____ Zip _____

SVT6-12/90

Please allow four to six weeks for delivery.
Prices and availability subject to change without notice.

SWEET VALLEY TWINS